# Sunday's Children

Works by Ingmar Bergman
published by Arcade

*The Best Intentions*
*Images*
*Sunday's Children*

# Sunday's Children

A NOVEL BY

# INGMAR BERGMAN

Translated from the Swedish
by Joan Tate

ARCADE PUBLISHING • NEW YORK

Originally published in Sweden by Norstedts Förlag, Stockholm,
under the title *Söndagsbarn*.

Arcade Publishing books may be purchased in bulk at special
discounts for sales promotion, corporate gifts, fund-raising, or
educational purposes. Special editions can also be created to
specifications. For details, contact the Special Sales Department,
Arcade Publishing, 307 West 36th Street, 11th Floor, New York, NY
10018 or arcade@skyhorsepublishing.com.

Arcade Publishing® is a registered trademark of Skyhorse Publishing,
Inc.®, a Delaware corporation.

Visit our website at www.arcadepub.com.

10 9 8 7 6 5 4 3 2 1

Library of Congress Cataloging-in-Publication Data is available
on file.

ISBN: 978-1-61145-863-3

Printed in the United States of America

# Sunday's Children

I REMEMBER THAT GRANDMOTHER and Uncle Carl were both critical of our summer house, though for different reasons. Uncle Carl was regarded as somewhat disturbed, but he knew more about various matters and declared the house was no house, definitely not a villa and under no circumstances a dwelling. The phenomenon might possibly be described as a number of wooden boxes painted red and placed side by side and on top of each other. Rather like the Royal Opera House, Uncle Carl thought.

Consequently and accordingly: some red wooden boxes with white corners and with arbitrarily placed and similarly white-painted moldings here and there. The windows on the ground floor were high and drafty and on the second floor square, rather like train windows: these were not drafty — they could not be opened. The roof was covered with worn and patched tar paper. When it rained heavily, water ran down the wall of the upper veranda and into Mother's room, loosening and buckling the floral wallpaper. This entire collection of boxes rested on twelve high stones, so between the lower floor and the uneven ground below was a space about two feet high. Within were weather-beaten gray pieces of wood, broken basket chairs, three rusty odd-shaped pans, some sacks of cement, worn tires, a tin bathtub full of defective household utensils, and several piles of newspapers bound with wire. You could always find something useful there. True, it was forbidden to crawl under the house. Mother thought we would injure ourselves on rusty nails or that the whole ramshackle structure might suddenly collapse on top of us.

A Pentecostal pastor in Borlänge had built this dwelling, or whatever it is to be called. His name was Frithiof Dahlberg, and he presumably wished to live in proximity to his Lord. So he looked for a place high above Dufnäs village.

He bought a plot below the hill and cleared the ground. In all likelihood, Pastor Dahlberg intended the Lord to appreciate his enterprise and provide him and his sons with some of the knowledge of the art of building they themselves lacked. Awaiting timely inspiration, they began, and in June 1902, after five years of adversity, the pastor's creation was completed. His parishioners admired his work and found certain similarities between Pastor Dahlberg's building and Noah's ark. Nor was Noah a qualified master builder but, strictly speaking, a good-natured, somewhat drunken barge skipper on the Euphrates. The Lord, however, had provided him with insight, and he had built a spacious boat that was to tolerate considerably greater strains than Pastor Dahlberg's modest dwelling.

Some of the pious thought the upper veranda, which faced south and had a view over the valley, the river, and the heath, was a fairly suitable place to await the Last Judgment, when the angels of the Apocalypse were to come racing across the hills over by Gangbro and Bäsna.

Just below the main building, the indefatigable pastor had put up a row of small outbuildings of unusual appearance. They consisted of seven cells welded together under a common roof, with a drafty green door leading into each cell.

These dwellings were presumably used by the kind of guests who wished to stay a few days or perhaps weeks, to be strengthened in their already unshakable faith by joint devotions and hymn singing. For lack of maintenance, the row had decayed and was now the haunt of much flora and fauna. The grass flourished through the floors, and a birch had made its way in through a window. Einar the badger, who had adopted the family, held court in the space on the extreme left, the field mice elsewhere, and an owl had at one time annexed the space with the birch but, unfortunately, had moved away. A semiwild yellow cat of malevolent appearance lived with six kittens in the most spacious cell. Mother was the only person who dared approach this bad-tempered creature. Mother had a special way with flowers and animals and defended our menagerie against all onslaughts from Maj and Lalla, who inhabited the two middle chambers. Lalla was our cook, and Maj was everything else. There will be more about them later.

This collection of buildings was complemented by an outsize but decaying privy, which raised its unpainted walls on the very edge of the forest. There was room for four shitters inside it. Through an unglazed opening in the door, you had a handsome view over Dufnäs, a section of the bend in the river, and the railway bridge. The holes were of various sizes: one, two, three, and a little wee one. On the lower back wall was a hatch that had fallen apart and couldn't be closed. When Maj and Linnéa visited this establishment for a little chat and a hurried pee, my brother and I partook in our earliest studies of female anatomy. We saw and were amazed. No one bothered to catch us at it. It never occurred to us to study our father or our mother or the overwhelming Aunt

Emma from below. Even the nursery has its unspoken taboos.

The furnishings of the house were heterogeneous. The first summer, Mother had a wagon loaded with disparate furniture from the parsonage in town. Grandmother provided additions from the attics and the cellar at Våroms. Mother plotted and planned, made curtains and wove a rug. She tamed this peculiar accumulation of disparate and internally hostile elements and made them get on together. The rooms, as I remember them, breathed a pleasing coziness. We really felt much better in Pastor Dahlberg's remarkable creation than at Grandmother's grand and tasteful Våroms, which was within a quarter of an hour's walking distance through the forest.

I mentioned in the beginning that Uncle Carl was fairly critical of "this haunt that is no house" and that Grandmother was also critical, but for other reasons. She regarded Mother's breaking away and renting the Dahlbergian creation as a quiet but declared rebellion. Grandmother was used to having children and grandchildren around her over the summer months, and for that reason she tolerated her son-in-law and daughters-in-law. This summer she was alone at Våroms with Uncle Carl, who for various reasons, not least financial, had no opportunity to rebel. Uncle Nils and Uncle Folke and Uncle Ernst and their families

had all gone to watering places abroad. So Grandmother was alone with Uncle Carl and Siri and Alma,
two elderly servants who disliked speaking to each
other, although they had worked together for over
thirty years. Lalla was also one of Grandmother's staff,
but she had suddenly declared that Mother needed all
the help she could get. She moved into Mother's
household at the beginning of July, and under primitive conditions she achieved masterly meatballs and
incomparable baked pike. Lalla had watched Mother
grow up, and her loyalty was unshakable though terrifying. Mother was not really afraid of anyone, but on
some days she did not dare go out to the kitchen to ask
Lalla what was for dinner.

The flat open space in front of the house was circular and graveled, enclosing a similarly circular lawn, in
the middle of which was a sundial, now rusted and
fallen to pieces. Outside the kitchen towered a great
bed of rhubarb. All of this was surrounded by a somewhat disheveled, never scythed meadow, stretching a
hundred yards to the edge of the forest and the decaying fence. The forest was thick and neglected, clinging
to the steep slope up toward Dufnäs hill; the precipice
leaned inward, and in thunderstorms the sound rever-
berated from it. In the gray and pink mountain there
was a deep cave, which could be reached after a highly
dangerous climb. The cave was forbidden and thus

tempting. A shallow stony stream wound its way around the mountain and past our fence, to disappear farther down under the fields and run out into the river north of Solbacka. In summer it almost dried up, in spring it was a torrent, in winter it murmured darkly and uneasily below thin membranes of the grayest of ice, while the autumn rains made it roar with a high, variable note. The water was clear and cold. Deep pools formed on the bends and in them could be found *kvidd,* a kind of carp, good as bait on long fishing lines in the river or Lake Svartsjön. The earth cellar had wild strawberries growing on top of it, and an ancient orchard languished on the slope below but still produced whiteheart cherries and apples. A steep path down through the forest led to Berglund's, the biggest farm in Dufnäs village, and from there we fetched milk, eggs, meat, and other necessities.

The narrow valley and precipitous mountain hillsides, the ancient forest and the rushing stream, rolling fields and then the river, cutting deeply into the ravine, dark and untrustworthy, the heaths, the hills — it was not exactly a romantic landscape but was dramatic and disquieting. Nature was not benevolent, nor even particularly generous. Yes, wild strawberries, lilies of the valley, linnaea, forest flowers, gifts of summer, but given sparingly and circumspectly. Thorny raspberry canes, a patch of vast, acrid-smelling bracken, tall clumps of nettles, dead and uprooted trees, huge boulders hurled by giants during some primeval period, poisonous fungi with no names but terrifying characteristics. For nine summers we lived in Pastor Dahlberg's dwelling, clinging on beneath the precipice right next to the primeval forest now beginning to encroach upon the meadow and the small patch of grass. If a storm came from the south-east and the wind raced over from the wide heath on the other side of the river, the ramshackle red-painted wooden boxes creaked, the drafty windows squealed and howled, and the curtains bulged ominously. Some child-lover had made me believe that the whole of Dahlberg's would rise and float away up toward the hill if the storm was fierce enough, the whole of Dahlberg's, with the Bergman family and the field mice and ants and all. Only those living in the row with Einar the badger and Lalla and Märta and Maj would survive. I never really believed all that, but whenever there was a really bad storm, I preferred to join Maj in her bed and command her to read aloud from *All for All* or *Allers Family Journal.*

Even in those days I had difficulties with reality, its limits unclear and dictated by adult outsiders. I saw and heard: yes, indeed, that's dangerous, that's not dangerous. There were no spooks: don't be silly, there are no ghosts, demons, corpses standing out there in full sunlight with wide-open bloodstained mouths. There are no trolls or witches. But down in the village at Anders-Per's place there was a horrible old woman imprisoned in a special little house with nailed-up windows. Sometimes when the moon was full and everything was still, you could hear her howls all over the village. And if there were no ghosts, why did Maj talk about the watchmaker from Borlänge, who hanged himself down at Berglund's? Or the girl who drowned one winter in the Gimmen and floated up in the spring down by the railway bridge with her stomach full of eels? I saw them myself as they carried up the corpse. She wore a black coat and had a winter boot on one foot, the other foot gone and the bone sticking out. She haunted me. I met her in my dreams, and sometimes I met her without dreams or darkness. Why do people say there are no ghosts? Why do they laugh and shake their heads, no, little Pu, you can be quite sure there aren't any ghosts? Why do they say that, when later they talk with such enthusiasm about things that really are horrible for someone with a far too thickly populated space behind his eyelids?

Now, quite briefly, we ought to talk about the Conflict. At this stage, which is the summer of 1926, it had existed for precisely sixteen years, its origins the theology student Erik Bergman's entrance into the Åkerblom family in his capacity as future husband to the well-guarded daughter of the house. Mrs. Anna did not approve of the alliance and expended her considerable strength of will on decisive measures. In himself, the future pastor might have been a mother-in-law's dream: ambitious, well brought up, tidy, and relatively handsome. In addition to that, the promise of a decent future in the service of the state. But Mrs. Anna had an eye for people. She saw something below the irreproachable surface: moodiness, oversensitivity, a violent temper, and sudden emotional coldness. Mrs. Anna also believed that she well understood her daughter, the family's bright and slightly spoiled central character. Karin was emotional, cheerful, clever, extremely sensible, and, as already mentioned, rather spoiled. Mrs. Anna thought her daughter needed a mature man, an obvious talent, a firm but prudent hand. That youth was already within reach of the family, Torsten Bohlin, lecturer in the history of religion. Everyone was agreed that Torsten and Karin were an ideal couple, and the parents were awaiting the announcement by the young people with confidence. Finally, Erik Bergman and Karin Åkerblom were second cousins, something considered a risky combination. Also, an indefinable hereditary disease lay concealed on the Bergman side, capriciously and appallingly afflicting members of the family: a gradual and accelerating atrophying of the muscles, which mercilessly led to difficult invalidity and early death.

So Anna Åkerblom considered Erik Bergman a clearly unsuitable husband for her daughter.

So did Johan Åkerblom, but for other reasons. He was already an old and sickly man and was devoted to his one and only daughter with an intense and resigned love. Every suitor was a conceivable and an inconceivable abomination. The old man wished to keep the apple of his eye as long as possible. Karin responded to her father's love with warmhearted if somewhat absentminded tenderness.

When the emotional relationship between the two young people became obvious, Mrs. Anna took to vehement and more or less well-calculated measures. Anyone interested in the matter can study a detailed documentary called *The Best Intentions.*

With good reason, Erik Bergman felt rejected and badly treated, and severe hostilities broke out between him and his future mother-in-law. Martin Luther has said somewhere that you have to be cautious with your pronouncements, "for words flown out cannot be caught on the wing." As far as I can make out, a great many such words flew out during those first years. Erik Bergman was thin-skinned and suspicious, nor did he forgive easily. He never forgot a real or imagined injury.

Karin Åkerblom was in many ways her mother's daughter. Her strength of will was undisputed. She had decided: she was going to live her only life with Erik Bergman. She had her own way, and the young novice priest was finally, reluctantly accepted.

From the announcement of the engagement onward, all the outward signs of conflict were buried. The tone became friendly and superior, courteously attentive, occasionally heartfelt, all the roles acted out. No one was to put familial unity at risk.

Hatred and bitterness remained, invisible and below. It was revealed in subordinate clauses and sudden silences, in imperceptible, absent, or strained smiles. It was all extremely sophisticated and kept strictly within the narrow confines of Christian forbearance.

One of the hypothetical complications was the summer. How was the summer to be organized? Where would the pastor and his family stay during the holidays? Mother had spent the summers of her childhood and youth at her parents' house in the heart of Dalarna. To her, it was obvious that her beloved should like Våroms, Dufnäs, Dalarna in the same way she did. Erik Bergman said nothing and submitted, wishing to please his young wife. Then the children came along, and they liked it at Grandmother's. Silence and courtesy, the silences and the subordinate clauses becoming more and more tangible as the idyll solidified.

Gradually, and possibly too late, Karin Bergman realized that this course was heading for disaster. One summer, her husband did not come, pleading a locum tenens for an ailing colleague. Another summer, Erik Bergman stayed briefly for a week or two and spent the rest of the time on a walking tour with friends. Yet another summer, he was suddenly taken ill and had to spend his holiday at the very grand Mösseberg, cared for tenderly by the family's benefactor, the immeasurably wealthy Anna von Sydow.

So Mother realized, if somewhat late, that something had to be done. Renting the Dahlberg creation was both a compromise and a silent prayer for forgiveness. The house was after all within walking distance of Våroms. The Bergman family would remain a family during Father's holiday. That Sunday dinners were to be at Våroms and that Grandmother would suddenly appear, usually unannounced, at the Bergmans' extremely primitive summer residence were inescapable complications.

Mother carried out the burdensome move with humor, receiving unexpected help from old Lalla, who that summer left her habitual and comfortable room behind the kitchen at Våroms and settled into our primitive row of outbuildings. Mother was her

13

darling and was to have all the help required. That was self-evident, but it shook Grandmother just as much as her daughter's rebellion.

Mother had little appreciation of her deed. When Father eventually appeared there in the summer of my eighth birthday, he was restless, absentminded, and melancholy.

DUFNÄS RAILWAY STATION consists of a red station house with white corners, a privy labeled MEN and WOMEN, two signals, two sidings, a warehouse, a stone platform, and an earth cellar. The stationmaster, Ericsson, has lived on the top floor of the station house with his goitrous wife for twenty years. The boy Pu, who is just eight, has his mother's and his grandmother's permission to be down by the station. Uncle Ericsson has not been consulted, but he treats his young visitor with absentminded friendliness. His office smells of ingrained pipe smoke and moldering linoleum. Sleepy flies buzz at the windows; occasionally the telegraph taps and emits a narrow strip of paper with dots and lines on it. Uncle Ericsson is leaning over his big desk, writing in a long book with black covers. After that he sorts out goods-consignment notes. Now and again, someone taps on the hatch in the waiting room and buys a ticket to

15

Repbäcken, Insjön, Larsboda, or Gustavs. The quiet is like eternity and certainly equally dignified.

Pu comes in unannounced. He is small, noticeably thin, almost scraggy, his hair cut extremely short, and he has scabs on his right knee. As this is Saturday afternoon at the end of July, he is wearing a washed-out shirt with the sleeves cut off and short trousers, his underpants hanging below them, the whole outfit held together by a scout belt with a sheath knife hanging from it. It may be hard to see what Pu is thinking. His gaze is somewhat sleepy, his cheeks childishly round, and his mouth half open, presumably from adenoids.

He courteously greets the stationmaster: Good day, Uncle Ericsson. Uncle Ericsson is gazing into his black book and hastily looks up; his pipe gurgles and sends forth a small cloud. Good day, young Mr. Bergman.

Pu climbs up onto one of the high three-legged stools by the telegraph.

"Father's coming on the four o'clock train."

"Is he now?"

"I'm to meet him. Mother and Maj are coming later. Maj has to fetch something or other."

"Oh, yes."

"Father's been in Stockholm, preaching to the King and Queen."

"How grand."

"Then he was invited to dinner."

"By the King?"

"Yes, by the King. Father's an old friend of the King and Queen. Specially the Queen. He gives her good advice and that sort of thing."

"That's good."

"The King and Queen probably couldn't manage without Father."

There is a long pause for thought. Uncle Ericsson lights his languishing pipe. A fly buzzes, dying in a shaft of sunlight. The fat mottled cat gets up and stretches its forelegs, purring. It takes a few staggering steps along the overburdened windowsill and lies down on top of *Sweden's Communications*. Pu screws up his eyes. The sunlight is burning white and immobile above the tracks and the tall birches. A small shunting engine coupled to a few lumber flatcars is asleep in the far siding.

"I think the Queen's in love with Father."

"Is she now. Fancy that now."

Uncle Ericsson does not sound particularly impressed, and he is also occupied with his consignment notes. The totals don't agree. He counts them again and again and puts them into two heaps — fifteen, sixteen, seventeen, eighteen. Someone knocks on the hatch into the waiting room. Uncle Ericsson puts his pipe down on the heavy ashtray, gets up, opens the little glass window, and says good day, good day. Oh, yes, all the way to Rättvik today? Aha, and to Orsa tomorrow? Aha. That'll be two seventy-five. Thank you. There we are.

Mother and Maj and brother Dag come strolling slowly out onto the sun-white sandy stretch. Mother is wearing a light summer dress with a wide belt around her narrow waist. Her hat is yellow and wide-brimmed. As usual, Mother is beautiful, really the most beautiful of all imaginable people, more beautiful than the Virgin Mary and Lillian Gish. Maj is wearing a fairly short faded dress in blue-checked material. She has black stockings and dusty black boots high above her ankles. Dag is four years older than his brother and is dressed much like Pu, with the difference that his underpants are not hanging down over his knees. Mother seems slightly cross and says something to Dag, frowning and smiling at the same time. Dag shakes his head and looks around, catches sight of Pu through the window and points at him. Oh, there you are, of course, says Mother with slight annoyance, but it's like being at the cinema: you have to guess what people are saying. She makes a sign to him to come out at once. Good-bye, then, Uncle Ericsson.

At that moment, the wall telephone rings two short

signals. The stationmaster takes the receiver and says: Hello. Dufnäs. Someone in the receiver says: Departed Lännheden two fifty-two. Uncle Ericsson puts on his uniform coat and places his uniform cap with its red cockade on his head, takes the flag from the blue stand inside the outer door, and goes out onto the station house steps, closely followed by Pu. They walk over to the signal, which soon raises its red-and-white-striped arm, and now the train can come. Uncle Ericsson salutes Mother and Maj, then goes over to a man with a horse and cart. They chat briefly and point at the warehouse.

Pu stays by the signal, keeping guard over it. Mother calls him, but when he doesn't hear or pretends not to hear, she shakes her head and turns to Maj.

The bright sunlight is blazing down on the warehouse and the station house, on the tracks and the platform. There is a smell of tar and hot iron. Over by the bridge, the river murmurs, the heat trembling above the oil-spotted sleepers, the stones glinting. Silence and expectation. The fat cat has settled down on the handcar. Discreet sighs come from the little shunting engine on the far track. Fireman Oscar has started lighting the boiler. Suddenly the train appears around the corner by Långsjön, first as a black blob in the heavy greenery, almost soundless, but soon with rising thunder. Now the train with its powerful compound engine and its eight coaches is out on the river bridge, the points crashing, the thunder deepening, and Pu's heart trembles.

The engine puffs and hisses, steam rushing out beneath the pistons, the ground shakes, and now the coaches are coming, long, elegant Stockholm coaches, brakes shrieking. Uncle Ericsson greets the driver with a salute. Pu is as if turned to stone. Now the stationmaster is waving his red flag. Everything screeches and creaks, in some inexplicable way everything has stopped and is still, while the engine snorts and snorts. Come on, Pu, Mother commands. It's best to obey when she uses that voice.

Father steps down onto the platform. He is still quite far away but is approaching with swift strides. He is bareheaded, and his thin hair is blowing about a bit. He has his coat over his arm and his hat in his right hand, in the left his shabby black briefcase bulging with books and his night things. Father hates luggage and likes to travel light. Mother and Father kiss each other on the cheek, knocking Mother's yellow hat sideways. They smile at each other, and now it's Dag's turn. He shakes his father by the hand, and Father pats the back of his head, rather roughly and less lovingly, one might think. Pu takes off and, laughing with delight, rushes at his father, who at once laughs

and lifts up his son and holds him hard in his arms.
Mother has taken over the hat and coat, and Maj,
discreetly curtsying, has relieved the pastor of his
bulging briefcase. Father smells of shaving lotion and
cigarillos, and his cheek is rather scratchy sharp. Give
me a kiss, Father says, and Pu plants a wet smack on
Father's ear.

Uncle Ericsson signals departure. The engine lets
out rhythmical black puffs of smoke, the wheels skid
and take hold on the track, doors and gates slam. The
signal is dropped, the train goes faster and faster on
its way to the viaduct across the road. On the bend
below Våroms, the engine hoots, then disappears into
the forest.

Must we go straight home? says Dag, turning
somewhat indecisively to the accumulated parental
authority. No, by all means, says Mother, smiling
quickly as she realizes that Dag's question is inappro-
priate at this moment. No, by all means. Only be
back in good time for dinner. You've got your watch,
says Father rather curtly. It's broken, but I can ask,
says Dag.

The forge is a few hundred yards north of the
railway station, a high, short, badly built, red wooden
building. The forge is on the ground floor, and the
upper floor consists of two rooms and a spacious
kitchen, and Smed the blacksmith and his wife,

Helga, live there with five children of various ages and accomplishments. Jonte is the same age as Pu, and Matsen the same age as Dag. Everything is filthy and wretched and poor all around Smed and his family, but as I remember it, the atmosphere is fairly cheerful. So we like going to the places by the forge to play. Smed the blacksmith looks like a Kirghiz chieftain. He is a handsome, dark-skinned man, his wife a stately woman with the remnants of worn beauty. She hasn't many teeth left, but she likes to laugh, and then she holds her big hand in front of her mouth. The hair and eyes of the whole family are as black as night. The youngest is a four-month-old girl named Desideria. She has a harelip.

As soon as Dag and Pu have managed to escape from the reception committee down at the station, they set off hurriedly for the strictly forbidden place behind the forge. Mother thinks they shouldn't play with the Smed children at all. Grandmother takes the opposite view, which is why they have permission to be together. Only one place is fenced-in, totally prohibited. That is the pool behind the smithy, an accumulation of water in a round hollow in the undulating meadowlands that stretch from the steeply sloping forested land down to the river and the ravines. In the spring that pool can be over six feet deep; in the summer it is considerably shallower. Tadpoles, carp, and one or two overweight sunfish flourish in the muddy water.

On this particular afternoon, there's a sea battle in progress out on the water. Two roomy crates, reasonably well sealed and tarred and painted with skull and crossbones on the makeshift prow, are a pirate ship and Queen Elizabeth's freebooter. Pu's brother Dag is the director and play leader of the war game. He has assigned himself the role of pirate chief. Matsen is General Archibald. General and pirate are alone in their respective craft. At an agreed signal, they hurtle out from each side of the pool and, with the help of a homemade oar, paddle at high speed toward each other. The collision is violent. After that the two combatants push and shove at each other with their oars. The battle appears to last for five minutes and is supervised by Matsen's older sister Inga-Brita, who has the Smed family alarm clock at her disposal. Whoever falls in the water has lost. If the boat can be capsized, the success is regarded as considerable.

Bengt, Sten, and Arne Frykholm from the Mission House are on Dag's side. The Törnqvist boys, perpetually sniffing and coughing, are on Matsen's. Despite permanent hostility, family solidarity demands that Pu be on his brother's side. As expected, the battle becomes embittered and, after a minute or so of ritual fencing, turns into uncontrolled hand-to-hand

23

fighting. Dag is the angry kind who fights over the slightest thing. After a few minutes, he has tipped over Matsen's boat and leaped out of his own. Standing in the muddy water up to their chests, the two parties start fighting seriously, making genuine efforts to drown each other, cheered on wildly by their respective adherents. As the battle rapidly degenerates, Helga Smed opens the upper-floor window and shouts that anyone who wants juice and buns must come at once. The audience immediately abandons the fighters, who stop for lack of attention and wade ashore. They take off their wet clothes but keep on their underpants, so Dag runs little risk of being discovered, and Pu does not dare tell on him.

It's crowded in the Smed kitchen. Two glasses and four cracked china cups are agreed on — the guests have priority — and the buns are freshly baked. A silent polite slurping ensues. The sun sends sharp shafts through the dirty window, the dust shimmers, the heat is terrific and the unfamiliar smells suffocating. Mrs. Helga lifts her latest born and gives her the breast, seated on the brown bed in the room beyond the kitchen. She pulls up a dirty dark-red blouse over her breast, and Desideria sucks eagerly. When the baby girl has had enough and belched, she is put down on the bed. Helga turns to my friend Jonte and urges him to come over to her: Come now, Jonte, and you can have yours. It is possible Jonte looks embarrassed; I don't remember, but I don't think so. Anyhow, he goes over to his mother and stands between her knees. She lifts her heavy breast and he drinks greedily. (Jonte has had consumption and been in a sanatorium all winter.) After he has slaked his thirst, he wipes his mouth with the back of his hand and munches on his rye bun and syrup. Helga is just about to pull her blouse down and get up from the bed, when Pu asks in a loud voice if he can have a taste. Everyone laughs, a loud laugh resounding around the hot, filthy kitchen. The woman also laughs, shaking her head: I've no objection, Pu. But I think you'd better ask your grandma or your mom first. They all laugh again, and Pu is embarrassed: his protruding ears redden first, then his cheeks and forehead, then the tears come; he can't possibly stop them. Helga Smed pats him with her hard hand and says that if he would like another bun, she'll spread the syrup on it. But Pu does not want a bun, and her bluff friendliness confuses him even more, the tears now running out of his nose into the corners of his mouth. Oh, shit, shit, shit! They all laugh a third time. Pu's a girl, really. You can see that quite clearly, says brother Dag. Pu throws his cup at his brother's face, and stumbling and furious, he makes his way down the steep stairs of the forge.

Maj is by the soot-covered window, talking to the blacksmith. He is to solder a saucepan that has cracked. A coal fire is burning on the forge; black wheels, levers and driving shafts, the scarred wooden workbench along the forge windows. The slippery rotting floor, patched with ends of planks and flat stones. The smell of burned coal, hot oil, and soot. Smed exudes his own smell, whatever that is. Anyhow, it's not a horrible smell, and Maj seems to like it. She is laughing at something the blacksmith has said and retreats slightly but not in an unfriendly way.

Maj turns her freckled sunburned face to Pu and, laughing foolishly, says they must hurry on back so as not to be late for dinner. She pushes a strand of hair off her forehead. The blacksmith nods at Pu, showing his teeth, which are white, as if new. Outside the forge, a gangling boy is waiting with a large horse that is to be shod. Hasty good-byes, and then Maj's bicycle. Pu clambers onto the carrier and clings to the saddle springs. Moving right in front of his nose are Maj's bottom, hips, waist, and back, and she smells of Maj. Pu loves Maj just as much as he loves Mother, sometimes more, but in a confusing way.

At the post office, the gravelly road runs up a short but steep hill. Maj keeps on for a bit but then gives up, and they walk side by side, helping to push the bicycle. You been crying? says Maj without looking at Pu. No,

I haven't, but I've been damned angry, Pu replies at
once. When I'm angry I look as if I've been crying, but
I haven't been crying. Was it Dag? Maj goes on to ask.
Pu thinks for a moment and says seriously: One day
I'll stick a knife into him. Pu draws in the snot in his
nose. He has almost recovered. No stabbing your
brother, says Maj, laughing. You'd be sent to a refor-
matory. Don't laugh, squeaks Pu, shoving Maj, and
she takes a step to one side. Stop pushing, you little
shit, says Maj in a friendly way, then: No, all right, I
won't laugh, I promise you. But you must learn that
people laugh at all sorts of things, and there's no
harm done. You can laugh too, can't you?

At exactly five o'clock, all the inhabitants of the
house are standing by their chairs around the dining
room table. Hands clasped, they say in unison: For
what we are about to receive, may the Lord make us
truly thankful. Then everyone sits down noisily, clattering and banging. The congregation is now assem-
bled, ten people in all. Mother and Father opposite
each other. Moster Emma sits enthroned on the right
of Father, and she isn't mother's sister at all but is
Father's father's sister, a leftover overweight dinosaur
from Father's family. We just call her Aunt. In the old
days in the countryside, *moster*, or mother's sister, was
a way of addressing older unplaced female relatives.
Aunt Emma usually lived alone in a twelve-room

27

apartment in Gävle. She was a glutton and horribly mean, nor was she particularly friendly, but sharp-tongued and witty. Christian duty prescribed summer and Christmas visits from Aunt Emma. She was gruffly tenderhearted and considerate to children, reading them stories and playing Ludo with them. Pu was Aunt Emma's favorite, and she liked to explain that he would one day inherit her fortune. Pu smiled ingratiatingly. He was probably a fawning child.

Lalla is on Father's left, as if sitting on a pin, for she sternly disapproves of Mother's democratic idea of gentry and servants all having summer meals together. I can't recall Lalla ever looking in any way different or special. A small, sinewy person with quick movements, a basically sensible face, a sarcastic smile, a broad forehead, her gray hair parted in the middle, deep-blue eyes. Lalla was the ruler of the kitchen. She had known Mother as a child and a young girl but still unshakably called her Mrs. Bergman.

Maj sits next to Lalla. She is in charge of Lillan, who is four and has just left the high chair for a hard cushion. Lillan was a round, friendly, and soft little person. When no one was looking, Pu liked to play with his sister. When Dag was anywhere near, he called her Porkie. As Dag hit Pu for the slightest thing, Pu hit Lillan for the slightest thing. Lillan sat on her round bottom, gazing with astonishment at her brother, her big blue eyes filling with tears. However, she seldom told on him. Pu preferred to be with his sister and play with dolls in the well-stocked doll's house than with his brother, who preferred playing with tin soldiers.

On the other side of Lillan is Marianne, a dark beauty, broad-hipped and high-bosomed. Father and Mother had been close friends of Marianne's parents, who were killed in a train crash. Marianne had been in Father's confirmation class and came often to the parsonage. This summer she was tutoring Dag in German and mathematics. He had no objections, as he was in love with his beautiful teacher. Pu was also in love with her, but from a distance, as he realized his inadequacy. At the same time, he envied his brother and teased him about his far too evident tender emotions. Marianne had a natural alto voice and wanted to be an opera singer.

Mother has Dag and Pu on her left, and Märta is next to Pu. Märta Johansson was a tall, thin woman of indeterminate age, rather fluttery and with a slight stoop. She was really a fully qualified primary school teacher but suffered from ill health: bad heart, only one lung. Her gentle temperament and soft image made her everyone's friend. Though Lalla did not like her, for Märta had once forgotten to turn off the gas stove one evening at the parsonage, thus causing a

29

minor explosion. According to Lalla, it would have been best if "that poor creature" had gone the same way. When Mother was away from the home with Father, Märta took over the housekeeping with good-natured determination. This summer she was in a delicate state of health and was visiting the family for rest and recreation. Pu could imagine an angel looking like Märta. She died a few years later and most certainly became an angel.

Saturday dinner menu is seldom altered. It consists of meatballs with macaroni in white sauce and whortleberry preserves. For dessert rhubarb fool is served, or strawberry fool, or gooseberry fool. The meal always starts with pickled herring and new potatoes, with which the pastor has a schnapps and a glass of pilsner. The rest of the family has small beer or, on Saturdays only, fizzy lemonade.

The dining room, which also serves as a living room, is spacious and light and adjoins a narrow glass veranda. Maj serves and Marianne helps whenever necessary. Märta is to be careful, and Lalla has orders to sit quietly and allow herself to be served, which she detests.

The potatoes for the herring are now being served, the dish goes around, Father pours the schnapps, and Aunt Emma also has a drop with her two pieces of herring and the pinkish thin-skinned potatoes. Do please enter the picture. You can stand there by the door out to the veranda or sit on the curvaceous sofa below the wall clock. At first we all talk at once, well-mannered and quietly. About the weather, of course: the weather in Stockholm and the weather in Dufnäs and the sudden heat, and Aunt Emma says there is thunder in the air and she can feel it in her knee, and in the same breath she says in knowledgeable tones that the meatballs are excellent. Lalla replies that she is glad Miss Eneroth appreciates the meatballs. As she says this, she smiles sourly. Neither praise nor criticism pleases Lalla, least of all from Miss Eneroth.

The only person who ever ventures a few careful words to Lalla with her Småland pride is the pastor. She likes that. That is quite in order. A mild admonition is invigorating to the soul. The ground is dry and the water in our stream has sunk a lot, Mother says. It's sad for the oxeye daisies and harebells. I've found a place, says Marianne brightly. There's a little meadow on the way to Lake Gimmen. There're lots of flowers and wild strawberries there. Dag and I were there the day before yesterday — no, on Tuesday. Really, outings in the middle of the week, my goodness, says Father jokingly. His forehead is slightly flushed from the schnapps. You should come too, Erik, says Marianne, as a diversion. It's a lovely trip.

The meadow's quite hidden. You can't see it from the road. That'd be nice, says Father, and smiles at Marianne. Alma was here this morning, by the way, says Mother suddenly. Siri came too, says Märta in her gentle, almost whispering voice. She showed me her handiwork. I'm going to do something similar. It's nice having something to do now that I've become so . . . sickly, so useless. She laughs.

You're looking much better, Märta, than when you came a few weeks ago, says Father, consolingly and kindly. Märta shakes her head slightly. Anyhow, Alma told us Ma is coming over for a while this evening with Uncle Carl. That's good, says Dag. Uncle Carl owes me two kronor, and I want it back. I'll give you your two kronor, says Mother decidedly.

Oh, so your mother's coming, is she? says Father, his forehead still a little flushed. Then we can bring in the gooseberry fool, Mother says, turning to Maj and Marianne, who at once get up and collect the meatball plates. Yes, Mother goes on, Mama is coming to talk about our joint excursion to Mångsbodarna, and she probably wants to wish you welcome home. Carl is coming because Ma doesn't like walking along the forest path alone ever since she twisted her ankle. Then we can see if Uncle Carl can shoot with a bow and arrow, says Dag. Father helps himself to gooseberry fool and pours milk into the deep plate with

garlands of flowers around the edge. It's strange, anyhow, says Father, shaking his head a little. What's
strange? says Mother at once. I think it's strange your
mother takes so much trouble to come here all the way
from Våroms. It'd be easier if we who're young and
quick took an evening walk through the forest. Yes, but
you know what Ma is like, Mother tries kindly. She's
probably bored over there in that big house.

Aren't any of her sons going to stay with her this
summer? I don't know, but anyhow that's the situa-
tion now, says Mother, frowning, her voice a trifle
curt. And what about dinner tomorrow? says Father.
Will that be as usual? What about it? As you know, as
I'm going to Grånäs to preach. I may not be back by
four, Father replies, and now he is looking at Mother.
But, Erik *dear*, I don't understand. Are you saying the
journey back from Grånäs will take *three* hours? That
can't be possible. Yes, it's quite possible, says Father,
his tone of voice light. That's perfectly possible, as I
can't escape the coffee hour. The minister writes *particularly* that he is pleased we shall meet after the
service. So I don't imagine I'll get away until about
two — and the freight train from Insjön, which I'll
catch, leaves just after half past three. I'm afraid you'll
have to say I can't come. Are you coming with me, Pu,
by the way? What! says Pu, his mouth gaping even
wider than usual. He probably hasn't been listening

very carefully. He doesn't like listening when Mother and Father use that particularly friendly tone of voice, and also he has grasped the content of the question, which constitutes a severe threat to his plans for the following day.

What? Well, little Pu, I'm asking you if you would like to keep your father company to Grånäs? Don't you think we might have a nice time? (Brief silence.) You should say yes, please, you'd like to, says Marianne, smoothing things over. Of course Pu would like to go with you, says Mother. Sure to be great fun, Dag says, grinning with undisguised malice. Father looks at his son Pu, who is struck dumb and is eating gooseberry fool and milk. You don't have to, Pu, his father says kindly. No, says Pu. Mother laughs lightly; she always modulates things. Have we finished, then? We all get up. We get up from the table, stand behind our chairs, clasp our hands against the backs: For what we have just received, may the Lord make us truly thankful. Amen. Bow and curtsy. Then you go up to Mother and kiss her hand and thank her for the meal, and then everyone helps clear the table, except Father and Aunt Emma, who go and sit out on the still baking-hot veranda among the geranium and Busy Lizzies.

Dag thrusts his face at Pu's. Fun, eh? Marianne catches hold of him and pulls his ears. Mind your own business or I'll give you math tests all day Sunday. Yes, wouldn't it be good if Dag shut up for once, complains Pu, who is truly burdened by the problem that has arisen.

Marianne grasps his shoulders and presses him to her soft bosom. I know Father would be pleased if you said you'd like to go with him. Pu shakes his head. He'd be much more pleased if *you* went with him. Marianne looks gravely at Pu. That can't be. Why not? It just can't, says Marianne, letting Pu go.

Don't run off now, cries Maj. You're to help with the dishes. Pu can dry the spoons and forks. She pulls Dag with her. I'm only going for a wee, cries Pu, and slips out behind Marianne. He ducks quickly across the sandy yard and up to the edge of the forest, where he stands behind the cherry tree but doesn't have a wee. He just stands there, secretly spying on the Dahlberg dwelling and its inhabitants.

He sees Father and Aunt Emma on the veranda, a glimpse of them behind flowers and creepers. Father lights his cigarillo and Aunt Emma takes her indigestion pills. There's also a glimpse of Mother for a moment in the open doorway to the stairs. She is holding Lillan by the hand. Is Pu there? she calls out, not waiting for an answer. Märta goes past in the dining room, with glasses and plates on a tray. She says something inaudible, and Mother replies that Pu should not show his bad temper in that unpleasant

way. I must speak to him. Lalla steps cautiously out
onto the kitchen steps, carrying a pail. We must keep
the doors closed, otherwise we'll let in lots of mosqui-
toes and flies. Marianne has gone upstairs and is
brushing her thick brown hair with fierce strokes, and
you can see she is singing to herself. Mother goes over
to the veranda, holding Lillan by the hand, on the way
picking up a big tattered rag doll. Maj is briskly washing dishes, talking all the time to Märta, but the
kitchen window is closed, so you can't hear what she is
saying. Dag has been armed with a tea towel and is
drying glasses. Märta helps with the drying, sitting on
a chair wiping plates. Märta laughs at something Maj
has said, and Maj shoves at Dag with her backside.
Marianne runs down the stairs and catches hold of
Lillan. She lifts her up and hugs her. Her arms are
bare. Lillan clutches the limp old doll. They go over to
the high carved piano, and Marianne sits down with
Lillan on her lap. They play note by note: first Lillan,
then Marianne. Mother stands by the flower table on
the veranda, turned toward Pu but not seeing him.
She is busy picking yellow leaves off a handsome geranium that leans its big red bloom against the dusty
windowpane.

The sun has moved behind the house, leaving the
veranda in bluish shade. The trees sough, and there's
a rustling and creaking in the aged branches of the

cherry. Pu has no defenses against a sudden grief. However, it does not last long.

Conversation can now be heard over by the rotting gate. Grandmother and Uncle Carl are there, panting after the taxing walk through the forest from Våroms. This provides an excellent opportunity to escape drying dishes, and Pu rushes across and down to the gate. Grandmother pats him on the cheek, and Uncle Carl shakes him, with a hard grip on the back of his neck. Carl smells of *punsch* liqueur. Pu knows it's the smell of *punsch,* as Mother always greets Uncle Carl with the same remark: I don't understand why you always smell of *punsch,* Carl. At which Carl replies that it might be due to the fact that he constantly drinks *punsch.* Uncle Carl has a trim beard, large blue eyes behind pince-nez, and soft fat hands, a big soft stomach with a watch chain across it, and he is wearing a white, somewhat grubby summer suit and a stiff collar and tie. He has a crumpled linen hat on his head.

Grandmother is short, but despite her small size she is almost imposing. She is sixty-two, her face round, and she has a goodly double chin; her eyes are blue-gray and piercing; her gleaming white hair is brushed back off her broad forehead. She wears a black full-length dress with a white collar and lace cuffs. A grayish-beige summer coat hangs over her arm. Grandmother has small round hands, which can be both soft and hard.

I think Pu's grown since yesterday, says Uncle Carl mockingly. Or perhaps it's his nose. Uncle Carl pulls Pu's nose. Pu is delighted. Uncle Carl is a favorite. Grandmother puts her stick on Pu's shoulder and takes his hand. If you come over tomorrow, we can read some chapters of *Treasure Island*. No, I can't, says Pu. Can't? No, I can't because I'm going to Grånäs with Father. He's going to preach in the church and wants me to go with him. Oh, really. Aha. That sounds like fun, mocks Uncle Carl. Grandmother gives him a brief look, so he says nothing more. We can read twice as many chapters next Sunday, says Grandmother, pressing Pu's hand.

Mother comes toward them, Father descends the veranda steps, and Aunt Emma shows herself in the inner doorway. Welcome to Dufnäs, Erik dear. I hope you'll have a lovely, restful holiday. Thank you, my dear Aunt. Thank you, that's very nice of you.

Hello, Carl, are you coming in for a brandy? Father pats Carl's arms. We haven't any brandy, says Mother emphatically. Now the rest of the family have come out, and they greet Grandmother with varying degrees of heartiness. Mother invites them over to the lilac arbor, where coffee and cake have been laid out.

I want to shoot with a bow and arrow, cries Carl. Is

there anyone brave enough to challenge me? I'll wager two kronor. He fishes out his great purse and extracts a shiny two-kronor coin and puts it on the cracked sundial base. How extravagant you're being, remarks Grandmother, laughing, and she sits down on the once-white garden chair. Aunt Emma, Mother, and Father join her. They immediately start arguing about the excursion to Mångsbodarna, which according to tradition takes place on the second Sunday in August.

Lalla has sat down on the kitchen steps and is drinking her coffee *au canard,* her knitting beside her. Märta is occupying the hammock with a novel, and Maj is readying the bedrooms for the night. She is whistling.

Besides Uncle Carl, Dag and Pu and Marianne are all taking part in the archery contest. The bow is a cross between a toy and a weapon, a fairly alarming object. The target is bulky and round, with colored rings around a black dot in the middle. It is placed against the privy door, and distances are measured. Pu gets a few yards in his favor.

We may not be able to come on the excursion this summer, Father's clear baritone can be heard saying. Mother says something that can't be distinguished, and Grandmother's smile is still steadily benevolent. The arrows bury themselves in the soft surface of the target. No, we won't be, Father's voice can be heard saying. Märta raises her eyes from her novel but returns to it. Lalla slurps a little. She has poured the hot coffee into the saucer and balances the saucer on the tips of three fingers. Uncle Carl shoots. Marianne applauds. Now it's her turn. Dag is prostrate on the ground, keeping score. Uncle Carl has lit a cigar and sat down on a stool forgotten in the meadow for several years and then left there. Pu has been given the task of fetching the arrows.

Terribly kind of you, Mother Anna, but your invitation doesn't really change anything, says Father. He is still the only one to be heard, although all of them are involved in a fairly lively conversation. Terribly kind of you, and I presume you think it very impolite, but I — *You* can say no on your behalf, says Mother, raising her voice, but I'm actually deciding, but what Mother is deciding can't be heard. A little breeze runs through the trees at this hour or so before sunset. A cow is lowing down at Berglund's pasture, and Sudd barks once or twice.

I see to my astonishment that I have said nothing about Sudd. He is a brown poodle of noble origins and according to his pedigree is called Teddy of Trasselsudd. In his childhood he ran away with his mother from a circus and landed in the dog pound, a collecting place for the city's stray canines. Father bought him for five kronor. He at once became a member of the family. Pu was afraid of Sudd, which Sudd immediately noted. He bit Pu when he could get at him. Pu retaliated. When Sudd was asleep, Pu poured water on him or shot off a cap in his ear. Sudd is now barking at Berglund's cow to maintain order.

Pu was to compete but can't really draw the bow. He can feel Uncle Carl's fat stomach behind his back. Wait, shall I help you? Pu is enveloped by Uncle Carl and his cigar smoke. He helps Pu draw the bowstring. Well, shall we? whispers Uncle Carl, with the fat cigar between his thick bluish lips. Shall we? What we shall Pu understands perfectly well. Uncle Carl and Pu hold the bow together, and now there's an arrow lying against the string. The arrowhead, though, is no longer pointing at the target but at the arbor. The sharp, steel-capped arrowhead searches: not Father, nor Mother. Pu closes his eyes and looks, closes his eyes again. Uncle Carl is breathing heavily; there's a rustling behind his tight waistcoat, and his stomach rumbles. Well, shall we? he whispers, and lowers a cloud of cigar smoke over Pu. Grandmother is sitting in profile, for the moment turned toward Aunt Emma. She is talking, her forefinger emphatically striking the edge of the garden table. Just think of at last silencing that old woman's eternally wagging tongue, whispers Uncle Carl.

Mother gets up to give Grandmother more coffee,

hiding Grandmother with her body. Suddenly the arrow whizzes off with a sharp whir and hits the bull's-eye on the target. Pu's won, my God! cries Uncle Carl, utterly against all the rules, and hands over the two kronor to the boy now gaping with astonishment. Shut your mouth, Pu, Uncle Carl says, pressing his soft hand under Pu's chin. You look stupid with your mouth open like that. And you aren't stupid, are you? Or are you?

Maj comes out onto the kitchen steps carrying an enameled milk can, which must hold three quarts. Pu, do you want to come and fetch the milk? she calls across the yard. Yes, I do, he calls back, tucking the two-kronor piece into his trouser pocket.

Maj walks quickly down the slope toward the forest, Pu half running beside her. She is wearing her blue linen dress; her red hair is braided, the pigtail reaching her waist. She walks with her head thrust forward, her little turned-up nose poking straight ahead as she whistles to herself. All of Maj smells good of sweat and a green soap called Palmolive. Arriving at the bridge over the stream, they stop. The water is flowing along silently and swiftly, small dark pools forming by the stones at the banks and whirling slowly. Sea grass sways, swirling around in the gravel streambed. Can you see any fish? says Pu. Be quiet now; it scares them off if we come stomping along. We'll have to wait awhile and keep quiet. Pu is on all fours by Maj, who is sitting on her heels. He cautiously presses against her hip, and she puts her arm around his shoulder. Suddenly the fast-moving water is filled with struggling, shimmering shadows. Beneath the shadows glides a heavy flattened figure with a scraped bare head, a bullhead garfish. A light chill rises from the stream, and Maj slips her hand down toward the shoal. It disappears in one violent common movement. Only the garfish is left on the sand at the bottom.

This was where the watchmaker hanged himself, whispers Maj. What? Maj glances at Pu and corrects him. You always say "What?" as if you hadn't heard, but you've heard perfectly well. Where he hanged himself? Fancy you not knowing that. Over there behind those two grown-together pines. Over there in all that scrub. Yes, he hanged himself. Everyone said he took his own life because he was betrayed in love, but that's not true. Why did he hang himself, then? I'm not sure; Lalla knows the whole story, so you'll have to ask her. Does he haunt? says Pu, a shudder of cold pouring through him, though whether from the chill of the stream or the proximity of this terrible deed is difficult to know. Does he haunt the place? Yes, they say he goes poking around in the scrub. There are fat adders in there, for that matter, so be careful and watch what you're doing.

43

Ghosts and adders, mumbles Pu to himself. *I've* never seen anything, says Maj. But I never see things like that. You have to be special to see spirits and ghosts and hobgoblins. My grandmother is clairvoyant; I'm not in the slightest clairvoyant — But *I* am, says Pu, because I'm a Sunday's child. Are you a Sunday's child? I didn't know that. Oh, yes. On the fourteenth of July, 1918, I was born at three o'clock in the morning. What have you seen, then? says Maj rather distrustfully. Quite a lot. Pu, you're showing off. You'll have to tell me sometime. That sounds terribly interesting. Maj splashes water in Pu's face and laughs. You're just showing off.

She gets up and sets off at full speed down the winding stony forest track. Pu half runs after her.

"If you like, I'll haunt you when I'm dead."

"What's the point of that?"

"I could tell you what it's like."

"What?"

"Well, over there on the other side."

"Thanks very much. But I've no desire to know."

"I can come very carefully. And in daylight."

"What's all this silliness, Pu?"

"I promise."

"If you're dead, you're dead."

"But what about the watchmaker?"

"Oh, those are just silly stories."

Maj drowned herself in the river a few years later. She became pregnant, and the father did not want to acknowledge it. She floated up one early-spring day down by the bend in the river, with a large bruise on her forehead. Sometimes I think about her and our conversation on the bridge over the stream. She has never haunted me. But then she had made no promises.

Berglund's farm is on both sides of the road. The farmhouse faces the forest; the barn, stables, outhouses, and cowshed face the fields stretching down to the river and the railway station. The eighteenth-century timbered house has a kitchen with a hearth for the stove, a large table, and two wooden sofas. On the other side of the porch is the dairy. In the loft, two small rooms abut a dark attic cluttered with generations of household utensils and articles of clothing.

The farmyard is wide and well kept. At the back is the ancient log cabin on stilts that has become the grain store. Opposite the old house is the relatively new "The Exception," with its glass veranda and an orchard behind.

Old Mrs. Berglund helps in the dairy. She is broad and thickset, has a cloth around her head and no teeth. The dairy is spacious but has only one window; the walls, floor, and ceiling are whitewashed. Along the walls are wide shelves of cheeses in various shapes. In one corner glints the hand-driven separator, and in the middle of the floor is the milk churn. Mrs. Berglund pours out the milk using a quart measure with a long handle and a hook on the end.

"We're slaughtering two calves this evening, so you can tell Mrs. Bergman and Mrs. Åkerblom that there's veal, Maj. And calf's liver. The pastor really likes his calf's liver. He came today, I heard the boy say. He was down at the station, and Ericsson said the pastor had come on the three o'clock train from Stockholm. Would young Bergman perhaps like a honey sweet?

Mrs. Berglund waddles on swollen legs over to a blue cupboard with painted flowers and figures. She opens it and takes out a china bowl of bulging yellow sweets that look like cushions. You can have two, says the old woman, breathing on Pu. Pu has never really seen such an ugly person before; not even Aunt Emma approaches Aunt Berglund's ravaged ugliness. Say thank you properly, reminds Maj. What? says Pu, and at once remembers. Thank you very much, he says, bowing slightly. He breaks two of the sticky sweets apart and at once puts them in his mouth, so that his cheeks swell like balloons. Good, aren't they? says Aunt Berglund quizzically, her eyes almost disappearing behind the wrinkles and brown protuberances. Cup of coffee, Maj? I've made some for the butcher's men. No, thank you; we must get back home, says Maj with a little bob. But thanks all the same. Is it nice when

Father comes home for the holidays? says Aunt Berglund, putting her hand on Pu's head. Pu nods. We're going to Grånäs tomorrow, and Father is going to preach. So I hear, says the old woman, pushing the lid back over the churn. Pity I can't get to the service in Grånäs, but it's too far. And the boys' Ford is in Borlänge for repairs. Mrs. Berglund comes with them to the porch steps but then goes into the kitchen to supervise the bulging coffeepot. Don't forget to give my regards to Mrs. Bergman and tell her about the veal, she urges, smiling toothlessly. No, I won't forget. Good night, Aunt Berglund. Good night, Maj, and good night, Pu dear.

The slaughtering is going on down by the cowshed. The first calf is already lying on a platform with its throat cut and the blood pouring into a tin vessel. Old man Berglund is holding the vessel and whipping the blood. The two younger men have fastened a halter to the other calf. A rope is knotted to the halter, and the calf is led out to the yard. The farmer has a sledgehammer half behind his back. The three smaller Berglund children are standing timidly around the place of execution. Young Mrs. Berglund is helping her father-in-law with the newly slaughtered calf.

Pu stands as if turned to stone in the yard. He has seen chickens slaughtered, which is quite fun as well as horrible: once a cockerel flew away and perched on

47

the shed roof, where it sat without its head and flapped its wings for several minutes before crashing down. But Pu has never seen the slaughter of so big an animal as a calf. The farmer hits the calf between the eyes with the sledgehammer, a dull crash. The calf leaps and dances; something brown runs down over the animal's eye. He receives another heavy blow and falls, at once gets up again but stands still, his mouth open. Then he receives a third blow, the forelegs fold abruptly, and he drops, floundering.

The wind in the cherry tree has slackened and dusk is falling, but the sky is suddenly swept clean and there is a fiery yellow above the hills in the west. The evening train to Krylbo hoots below Våroms and gets its breath back at the station, smoke rising straight up out of the engine funnel, but he can hear it puffing and blowing and hear Ericsson's voice. He is talking to a railwayman as he rolls up his flag.

In the Dahlberg dwelling or "The Creation," as Uncle Carl calls it, the paraffin lamps have been lit in the dining room, in the kitchen, and on the lower veranda. In Mother's room upstairs, a night-light is burning for Lillan, as she is easily frightened by the dark. If you stand by the privy and look at the house, or whatever it is called, it shimmers from within and without, looking almost like an enchanted dwelling in a saga or a dream.

The adults have gathered around the dining room table, now lit by two lamps, one in the ceiling and one on the table. Mother is embroidering on a ring, Father reads the daily paper, both of them wearing glasses, Mother's always far down her nose. Aunt Emma is playing patience. Märta is leaning over her sketchbook and with thin watercolors paints a stern picture of some linnaea. Marianne is reading a thick biography of Richard Wagner, a pencil in her hand, with which she occasionally underlines something.

Dag and Pu are in the kitchen, each holding crispbread with soft goat's cheese on it and drinking milk, which is still warm. Lalla is also at the kitchen table, darning a stocking. She has unlaced her high boots and slipped her aching feet into soft slippers. Despite the suffocating heat, she has hung a woolen cardigan over her shoulders. Her spectacles are round, with narrow steel rims. The last cup of coffee of the day stands beside her on the table.

"Tomorrow's the Feast of the Transfiguration," Lalla informs them, as if the Bergman brothers ought to be interested in such events. "Tomorrow is the Transfiguration of Christ, Dag," she says again. "And there's something special about that day."

"What?" Pu asks out of politeness.

"It's the day God speaks to the Apostles. They hear a voice like thunder from the clouds, saying: 'This is

49

my beloved Son, in whom I am well pleased. Hear ye him.' God meant that Jesus was his beloved son. There must have been some people who doubted it."

"What's so remarkable about that?" says Dag, slurping into his glass.

"Where I was born and brought up, the Feast of the Transfiguration is special."

"In what way special?" says Pu, who is beginning to be interested, though he doesn't really want to be.

"For instance, you can be told how long you're going to live. Anyone going out into the sunset to a place where someone's taken his own life, he can find out this, that, and the other. That was quite certain back home with us."

"Have you tried, Lalla?" says Dag ironically.

"Not me, but my half sister has."

"Well?"

"I'm saying nothing. But it was remarkable, all right. She was a Sunday's child, by the way."

"What?" says Pu, his jaw dropping.

"I'm a Thursday's child and can see through clothes on pretty girls," says Dag confidently.

There's a crunching of crispbread and a slurping of milk. Lalla smiles, her false teeth fine and even. She has a bright smile that goes right up to her blue-gray eyes.

"You never know what's true and what isn't about

things like that. Pu sees differently from Dag. The pastor sees differently from Miss Eneroth. I see things Maj doesn't see. Everyone sees for himself."

"Why did the watchmaker go and take his own life?" says Pu quite suddenly. He asks though he doesn't want to ask, but now the question has been asked.

"No one knows for sure," says Lalla, looking as if she knew.

"You can tell us, Lalla."

"Then Pu'll be scared and wet himself," says Dag.

"Shut up," says Pu, rather impatiently, though not unkindly.

"No one knows for sure," says Lalla again. "But they say — I've heard it said — that he went mad with *fear*. He didn't come from here but from Tammerfors in Finland. At first he settled in Kvarnsveden, but no one there was interested in clocks, so he didn't do well. When his wife died of typhus, he moved to Borlänge, and quite a lot was going on there in those days, so he did well. But people thought he was peculiar. Oh, he was always friendly and polite, so it had nothing to do with that. And he did his work properly and was quite certainly an honest man, but nonetheless people thought he was a bit peculiar."

"Why did he take his own life?" Pu scratches a mosquito bite at the back of his knee. He has stopped munching on his crispbread. Even Dag is reluctantly though skeptically interested. Lalla now sees that she has captured her audience and is in no hurry.

"There was a grandfather clock in his shop, tall and narrow and black, with decorations in gold around the clock face. You could open a little upper hatch, where the pendulum was, and then — for some reason — there was a lower hatch as well. Inside, there was an empty space — or it *looked* empty. The clock ticked thoughtfully and with dignity and struck the half hour and the hour with a gloomy note. For many years there was nothing unusual about that clock; on the contrary, it kept good time and never needed repairing. But then suddenly — yes, from one day to the next — it seemed to change out of all recognition. It started going in both directions, sometimes several hours a day. And when it was to strike two, for instance, it struck seven. And when it was to strike on the hour, it struck on the half hour, and sometimes it just stood there deathly silent but started going again without the watchmaker having to start it up again. This clock business became a serious worry to the watchmaker. He repaired it and changed the mechanism and the cogwheels and weights and pendulum and hands. But that made no difference. In the end, he moved the clock into his back room, which was both kitchen and bedroom, a dark hovel behind his shop. He couldn't very well let this troublesome and disorderly clock stand there in the shop to become a laughingstock. He just couldn't. You can understand that. In that way, he lived with the clock both day and night. Several times a day, he closed his shop and rushed into the back room to check whether his clock had come to its senses. At night he woke every hour and listened to it striking, but he realized that everything was all wrong. One day, when he had taken out the works to examine the mechanism, a cogwheel leaped out as if of its own accord and sliced deeply into the palm of his hand. He bled terribly, and blood ran all over the works and down onto the table where he usually ate. He had to trot off to the local hospital to stop the bleeding and get the cut tended to.

"One night, he woke with a start as his clock struck thirteen, or perhaps it was fourteen, times, although it was four o'clock in the morning. It was winter and dark, yet there was a peculiar light in the room, and the light seemed to be gathered around the bottom part of the clock, a peculiar light, neither like dusk nor like dawn.

"The watchmaker sat up in bed and stared."

Maj comes pattering into the kitchen in her bare feet. She puts a flowered teacup with no handle on the kitchen table. It's full to the top with ripe wild strawberries.

"Maj! Where did you find wild strawberries at this

time of year?'' says Lalla in astonishment, possibly grateful for the interruption, as she realizes her performance will benefit from an intermission. Perhaps she has painted herself into a corner with her watchmaker, and now she has to find a way out.

"Above the old mill. There're always wild strawberries there twice a year. I went to see just for fun, really. There were lots there. But then it got too dark."

"Have a cup of coffee, Maj. There's a drop left in the pot. . . ."

"We're talking about the watchmaker," Dag informs her.

"Oh, are you — *that* story. Isn't it a bit awful for Pu at this time of night?"

"Oh, I'm not afraid."

"How do you know all that about the watchmaker?" says Dag.

"During the last years of his life, the watchmaker lived in a little backyard house at Anders-Per's on the road to Solbacka — some way away from here. And Anders-Per told your grandmother that the watchmaker had left a letter behind him with 'To be opened after my death' on the outside. Though of course no one knows for sure, for only Anders-Per has read that letter, and it disappeared when the old man died and the young ones sold the old man's escritoire at auction."

"Tell us," urges Pu, already shaken.

"Well," says Lalla, with renewed energy. "He saw that the lower hatch in the clock started opening all by itself. And out of the darkness inside came a peculiar noise. It was almost like someone crying, I imagine. But there was nothing to be seen. The watchmaker felt an indescribable terror. But he couldn't stay in bed. He lit a candle on his bedside table with a trembling hand, got out of bed, and padded over to the clock. He had the candle in his hand but was so agitated he had forgotten his slippers, and he noticed the floor was icy cold, for the fire had gone out and the room was freezing."

"You can understand that," says Pu, his teeth chattering.

"Oh, yes. But when the watchmaker crept up to the clock, he at once noticed the pendulum was swinging more slowly than usual, sagging and hesitating and seeming to stop, but it didn't stop. Both the hour hand and the minute hand had fallen down, and both were pointing at the six. The top hatch was closed, but there was a creaking in the bottom hatch, which was opening even further. The watchmaker fell to his knees in his long nightshirt and opened the door wide and shone the candle inside the dark space. At first, of course, he could see nothing at all, but when his eyes had got used to it, he found a small hatch inside the hatch, and that hatch had opened a little bit. And then he saw who was crying. It was a tiny little creature, a woman sitting curled up in there, sobbing terribly. She was wearing a long shift, and her thick black hair was spread out over her shoulders. The watchmaker noticed that the clock had stopped altogether, and now all he could hear was the woman's wretched sobs and the wind in the chimney. He reached out his hand and touched the little person. Though at most a foot and a half tall, she wasn't a child or a dwarf but a real woman. He touched her, and she looked up; she had hidden her face behind her hair and hands. But now, as she looked up, he could see her face.

"She had great blind eyes with nothing in them, just bluish whites. Her mouth was half open, and he could see no teeth because her mouth was bloodstained and her lips were bloody. Her face was thin and pale, almost emaciated, but she had a high forehead and her nose was narrow and refined. The watchmaker thought the little woman was the most beautiful person he had ever seen in all his life, although she was so confoundedly small."

"He fell in love with her, of course," says Maj.

"I don't know whether he fell in love exactly, but something did happen to the poor watchmaker." Lalla sighs, pulling her darned stocking off the darning egg. She smooths the stocking on the table and runs her hand over it.

"What then?" Pu urges her on, impatiently and terrified.

"Well, he lifted the little lady out of her prison and bathed her mouth and forehead with a damp cloth, wrapped her in a shawl, and put her on his bed. He lit the paraffin lamp and lay looking at the woman, who had closed her eyelids over her blind eyes. Presumably she was sleeping. He hadn't lain there long when the big black clock started creaking and shaking as if it had gone mad. Again and again it struck, but only once at a time and irregularly. It grew into a *horrible* uproar. There's no other way of describing it. Both hatches, the upper and the lower, kept opening and closing with violent crashes, and the pendulum swung hither and thither. The watchmaker realized the clock was furiously angry and was about to kill him. So he rushed into his workshop and fetched the steel hammer with a heavy lump on one side and a sharp edge on the other. Then he set upon the clock and smashed it to pieces. As he smashed the dial with a single blow, the clock fell over toward him with all its weight and size — it was taller than the watchmaker, who was a wiry little man. But the watchmaker got away with a cut on his foot. Just before the clock fell, just as the dial was smashed by the watchmaker's hammer, he seemed to glimpse a distorted evil face behind the cogwheels and rods. An evil, wide-eyed face with blind bulging eyes and a wide-open squealing mouth, full of rotting teeth. The face had a great gash on its forehead, and blood was pouring out. It must have been terrible, but it was to be even more terrible." Lalla empties her cup of coffee and scoops the sugar out with her spoon. Maj, Dag, and Pu wait breathlessly and attentively. No interrupting now.

Well, that was *that*," says Lalla eventually, after a well-calculated silence. "The watchmaker smashed his clock to pieces and perhaps also smashed that creature who lived in the clock. But that's not so certain. It's a guess. Nothing was written about that in the letter the watchmaker left behind him. While the clock was being smashed, the little woman wailed and howled like a madwoman, not human cries but those of an animal, a fox in a trap or something like that. The watchmaker tried to console her, but in vain. She screamed and screamed. He pressed her to him. He stroked her. He spoke to her. Perhaps he even proposed to her — I don't really know — but she just screamed and screamed and the watchmaker grew more and more desperate and wept and prayed as if for his life. And a matter of life and death it certainly was. Well, then the woman started grabbing at his hands, but she was blind, so he managed to protect himself. Suddenly she wrenched herself out of his arms and rolled down onto the floor and scrambled away on all fours. The table with the oil lamp on it tipped over, and one corner started to burn — I don't know, there was nothing about that in the letter. But the watchmaker flung himself after her and caught her and held her and kissed her, but she bit his lips, yes, it was a terrible fight, and you can't really talk about everything that happened in that battle. In the end, the watchmaker got hold of his hammer and smashed the woman to pieces just as he had smashed the clock to pieces. He was almost out of his mind. When he had calmed down, he dug a hole in his garden and buried both the woman and the clock. A few days later, he moved out of the shop and the house in Borlänge and settled down with Anders-Per on the road to Solbacka. Less than a year later, he had hanged himself."

Dusk thickens outside the yellow circle of the oil lamp, and a little moth bangs against the glass. From the next room they can hear Marianne singing. No one is accompanying her, and she is singing one of Jonas Love Almqvist's *Songes*.

> Dear Lord, how beauteous it is to hear
> the notes from a blessed angel's mouth.
> Dear Lord, how lovely it is
> to die in notes and song.
> Run still, oh my soul, in the river,

in the dim heavenly purple river.
Sink still, oh my blissful spirit,
into God's embrace, so fresh and good.


Dag gets up silently and puts his emptied glass on the drainboard, then he disappears, the door into the dining room opening and closing soundlessly.

"Dag's in love with Marianne," says Pu.

"A little shit like Pu can't understand that sort of thing," says Maj, pinching Pu's ear.

Pu is delighted.

"Yes, I can. He's said so himself. He says he's going to be an opera singer, just like Marianne."

"Pu, you shouldn't tell tales on your brother. That's not kind." Lalla gets up and packs her plaited raffia sewing basket. "Anyhow, Pu should go to bed now."

"I'm allowed to stay up till half past nine."

"Who has said that?"

"Grandmother said so."

"Aha, that's at your grandmother's, but now we're here at the Bergmans', and here it's nine o'clock."

Sighing, Pu gets up from his chair, thinking about the next day. A lot is going to happen on the Feast of the Transfiguration. He is to go to the suicide place at sunset and see if he can meet the watchmaker, and he has to go with Father to Grånäs Church.

"What's the matter, Pu? Don't you feel well?"

"What?" says Pu, his mouth open.

"Shut your mouth, Pu. I asked you if you didn't feel well." Maj looks down at the small figure.

"Hell, yes, I'm all right." Pu sighs. "But it's all so *much*."

"Come on. Let's go and listen to Marianne for a while, and then I'll make sure you go to bed, Pu. Come on, don't stand there with your mouth open. You must think about keeping your mouth shut. You look stupid like that."

"I know. It's only idiots who stand around with their mouths open."

"G'night, then, Pu," says Lalla. "And think about being a Sunday's child."

"Mm." Pu nods, burdened and chosen. "Mm."

"G'night, Maj. I'm off now."

"G'night, Miss Nilsson."

"G'night, Pu."

"G'night, Lalla."

Lalla disappears down the kitchen stairs to the row of cramped cells. Maj takes Pu by the slim back of his neck and pushes him ahead of her into the dining room.

Marianne is singing in the twilight. The lamps are out, leaving only a couple of candles on the big sideboard to light up the room. She is sitting on the piano stool, leaning forward a little, her hands in her lap. Her eyes are dark and wide open, and she is singing in a voice that is a living presence in her body. I am in love with her too, Pu thinks sorrowfully.

Mother is at the dining room table, her head in her hand and her eyes closed. Pu sighs. I am in love with Mother more than anyone. I want her to breathe on me, but at the moment I daren't go over to her. No, perhaps I'd better let her be. Pu sits down on a high-backed chair by the door into the hall. Lillan comes pattering down sleepily from upstairs. She has Baloo the teddy bear in her arms. Pu gathers her up on the threshold and lifts her onto his lap. She lets herself be held and at once puts her thumb in her mouth. The long eyelashes tremble against her cheek, and she leans against Pu, who likes sitting in the dusk with his sister in his arms.

Father has pushed his chair back from the table and his glasses up on his forehead, shading his eyes with his hand. He has undone his left boot, and his big toe is wriggling in his sock. Aunt Emma is asleep in her comfortable chair, with a cushion behind her head. Her mouth is open, and she is snuffling, on the border of snoring. Märta's eyes are gently still and sorrowful. She is cold despite the hovering, remaining warmth. Her cheeks are red. She must have a fever.

DAG AND PU INHABIT A ROOM that, because of the house's lack of any kind of plan, is the shape of an endlessly extended closet of about twice seven yards. The ceiling slopes, and you can't stand up straight by the four square windows unless you are shorter than three feet six. Two wretched iron beds with sagging bases stand in a line along the long wall. A folding table is folded down between the windows. Two odd chairs and a ramshackle cupboard with a mirror complete the furnishings.

Pu is asleep, or maybe he is not. Dag is reading a book with red covers, possibly only looking at the photographic illustrations. A candlestick on a chair provides a moderate light. Pu looks up.

"What are you reading?"

"Mind your own business."

"Is it that book full of naked women?"

"Come on, you can have a look. But it'll cost you five öre."

Pu immediately gets five öre out of a cardboard box.

The brothers absorb themselves in the red book called *Nackte Schönheit*. Dag has been learning German for two years, so he knows what it means. The pictures are of ladies and gentlemen posing, running, leaping, doing gymnastics, drinking coffee, and singing around a bonfire. All of them are naked. Dag points: That one's got a passable wig on her cunt. Did you ever see such a bush? The picture is of a thin woman just about to do a back handspring. She appears against a strong light. I like this one better, says Pu, concentrating on a plump girl leaping straight at the camera. I think she's like Marianne.

"Go to hell — she *isn't*."

"But it's good," says Pu, his cheeks growing hot. "It's really good. You could bite her."

"You're nuts," says Dag, slamming the book shut. "It's not good for you to look at pictures like these. We must go to sleep now."

"Who gave you the book?"

"I wasn't given it. I bought it, idiot."

"Who from, then?"

"From Uncle Carl, of course. I had to pay one fifty.

Uncle Carl never has any money. He'd sell Grand-mother if he could."

"Do you think you'd get anything for Aunt Emma?"

"You'd have to pay to get rid of that bitch. Though Lalla might bring in a bit."

Silence and darkness for a few minutes.

"Dag?"

"Shut up. I'm asleep."

"Do you think Maj screws with Johan Berglund?"

"Shut up. She screws with Dad. You know that, idiot."

"With Dad?"

"I don't want to talk. Shut up."

"But what about Marianne? Isn't she the one who screws with Dad?"

"She does too. You know perfectly well Dad's screw-crazy. He jumps on all women except Lalla and Aunt Emma."

"Does he screw with Grandmother too?"

"Of course, but only at Christmas and Easter. Now shut up."

A faint rhythmical creaking is coming from Dag's bed. Pu thinks of saying something, but passes. He's not quite sure what his brother is doing, but he presumes it's something awfully forbidden.

"Dag?"

"Shut up, for Christ's sake."

"Do you think Dad and Mum are screwing right now?"

"Do you want a beating?"

Some silence. The measured creaking increases.

"Dag?"

"Uh."

"What are you doing?"

No reply. The bed falls silent.

"Dag? Are you asleep?"

No reply. Pu falls asleep almost at once, for lack of a conversational partner. At last, the uneasy inhabitants of the Dahlbergian dwelling are all asleep.

A night wind comes down from the mountains and rustles in the pines, the cherry tree, and the rhubarb bed. Fine rain falls onto the hot tar-paper roof but stops almost at once.

The stairs creak, and Aunt Emma is standing in the doorway of the boys' room. She is attired in a long cardigan over her shift, has a crocheted cap on her head and her hair braided into a hard gray stump of a pigtail. She is breathing heavily with the strain of the stairs.

"Are you boys asleep?"

Mumbling, sleepy growling.

"I have to ask one of you boys to help me."

66

"What?"

"I have to go to the privy."

"What?"

"I must go to the privy at once. Someone must come with me to hold the lantern and support me. I can't go on my own, because then I'll fall."

"Can't you go in the pail, Aunt Emma?"

"I have to go *bigs,* you see, Dag."

"Can't it wait until tomorrow morning, Aunt Emma? Then Maj or Märta would help."

"I can't wait, you see, Dag. I ate half a box of figs last night. Oh, I've got such a stomachache, and it presses so."

"*I* can help you, Aunt Emma," says Pu kindly. He immediately gets out of bed and thrusts his feet into his sandals. Dag turns to face the wall.

"You're kind to your old aunt, Pu dear. You'll have a krona for your trouble."

"Of course, I can come if you absolutely have to go," says Dag, sitting up.

"No, thank you. You just go on back to sleep. Your old Aunt Emma doesn't want to be any trouble."

So the procession is on its way. Pu goes first, with the old stable lantern in his left hand. His right hand has a firm hold on Aunt Emma's fat little hand. Aunt Emma moves cautiously, putting one foot in front of the other, gasping with the effort and her stomachache.

67

Now and again, she stops on the gentle slope, a blanket over her shoulders. It's still drizzling, but the warmth of the day's sun wafts up off the grassy slope and the stones on the path.

They at last reach their destination. The lantern is put on one of the lids over the privy holes, and the old lady settles herself, groaning, over the widest hole. Pu sits outside on the steps, scratching a mosquito bite, the door left open for safety's sake. Aunt Emma's gigantic stomach rumbles and gurgles; dull, redolent farts trumpet into the stillness of the night. Heavy breathing and gasping go on behind Pu's thin back, and he can hear heavy, splashing thumps from the barrel and then the sharp sound of a rushing flow of water. She pees like a horse, thinks Pu. He cautiously holds his nose between his thumb and forefinger, discreetly so that Aunt Emma shall not see and be embarrassed. Then silence falls.

"Have you finished, Aunt Emma?"

"No, no. Don't hurry me."

"We can sit here all night if you want to, Aunt Emma."

"You're a nice little boy, Pu."

"Have you got a bad stomachache?"

"I don't really know. Yes, it's still there. I don't know, Pu. I'm so miserable. Your Aunt Emma is miserable all over. All that constipation and diarrhea, nothing is ever right. Sometimes I think that both my intestines and my stomach, my soul too, for that matter, are going to fall out, and I think maybe I'll die. But then I think about all the food I stuff into myself, and I swear I will be careful in the future and not eat what I can't tolerate. But the next day I break my promise, and then everything goes wrong again. Oh, oh, oh, oh, now it's starting again. I think I'm going to die."

Muted trumpets and dull thumps on muffled drums. The vast figure, lit faintly by the flickering flame of the stable lantern, rocks, curls up, and straightens, the fat legs dangling, elbows pressed into her sides. Oh. Oh.

"And now it's starting to bleed, of course. Those horrid hemorrhoids that never close up. I'll have to use my nightcap to stop the bleeding. Why can't the Bergmans rise to proper toilet paper? Why does the pastor use newspaper? I'd gladly pay. Ah, now it's starting again, and just as I —"

The panting stops. Pu can't hear if Aunt Emma is still breathing. He turns around. Suppose Aunt Emma is sitting there dead, staring at him with wide-open dead eyes? That would be really scary. But she isn't dead. All that's happened is that the old lady has covered her face with her hands. She is sitting upright, her nightgown hauled high up above the huge thighs, her hair in disorder since she has snatched off her nightcap, her face in her hands, and she is sitting there rocking silently. Perhaps she's crying?

"Are you miserable, Aunt Emma?"

"Yes."

"Why?"

"It's hell, Pu, my dear."

"What is?"

"Yes."

She takes down her hands, and Pu can see the tears shining like little rivulets on the slack cheeks. She bends her head and fingers the lantern. The shadow on the wall rises immeasurably. Then she starts speaking in a special voice.

"Old age is hell, you see, Pu, my dear. And then you die, and that's not much fun, either. And everyone will be relieved and will inherit a little money and some furniture. And it was good for the old girl that she could finally go. She never cared about anyone at all. So she was alone! But she ate herself to death, and that's the truth. Though she could brew good Christmas ale, no one can deny that."

Aunt Emma rustles newspaper, makes appropriate use of the nightcap, pulls up her long pink bloomers, then drops her nightie. Pu helps her down the two steps from the privy throne. The hand she holds out to him is cold and moist. She pats Pu on the head, a clumsy gesture. A faint shimmer of dawn is already visible just above the mountain and the edge of the forest.

Pu is sleeping the sleep of the exhausted. Perhaps he is dreaming he is flying, or that he is very small and is lying naked on Maj's stomach, or that he at last has the power to kill. First he will kill his brother, and then he has to kill his father. But first Father is to pray and weep and scream with fear. But he has to die, that is unavoidable. The king has ordered Pu to kill Father, so there's nothing to argue about.

Someone has said that fear makes manifest that which is feared. That's a good rule and also applies to small children, like Pu, for instance. Ever since the previous winter, he has nourished a recurring anxiety: that Father and Mother no longer want to be together. This has come about from Pu's being unwilling witness to a brief physical struggle between his parents. When they found they were observed, they stopped struggling at once and worried about Pu, who could not help weeping with terror. Father had a scratch down his cheek. Mother's hair was disheveled and her lips were trembling, her eyes were dark and her nose was red. His parents energetically explained that adults could be just as furious as any child. All this talk and explanation made no difference. Pu became more and more frightened as time passed. His fear

71

came gradually, and he started looking particularly closely at Mother and Father. He saw that they occasionally acquired special faces and special voices. Father turned white, his eyes went pale, and his head shook almost imperceptibly. Mother smelled of metal, and her soft, warm voice was curtailed, as if it hadn't enough air. Pu talked to his brother about it, but Dag looked scornful and laughed: To hell with those two. As far as I'm concerned, they can go to hell. The main thing is to be left in peace and that that damned thug who maintains he's my father stops thrashing me with the carpet beater. Pu said nothing and continued on his own. The problem remained.

He wakes now out of his deep sleep. It feels like a light blow in the solar plexus. He is confused and doesn't know which side of reality he is on: in his own, the reality governed and well controlled by Pu himself, which is indeed mingled with strange images and figures but nonetheless is his own and easily recognizable, or in the other reality, terrifying and new, now beginning to invade his mind and emotions. A second after waking up, he knows what has jerked him out of his dreams. He can hear voices from Mother's room: low, sometimes whispering voices. It is Mother and Father, involved in some kind of conversation. He recognizes their voices, or rather their voices remind him of earlier moments of sudden terror; what the *hell* is it this time? What are these whispering, gliding, alien tones in the middle of the night? Pu's teeth chatter. It's damned awful. I must listen properly. I must listen outside their door, so that I can hear properly what they're saying. Pu gets out of bed and puts his bare feet on the linoleum. It is cold and he shivers, although the warmth has not left the long, narrow room.

He at once sees that the door to Mother's room is half open, and he takes up a suitable position on the landing: he can see without being seen. Mother is sitting on the bed, her arms around her knees, her nightgown slipped down over one round shoulder; Mother hasn't braided her hair for the night. The heavy dark hair is floating about her shoulders, and her face is pale in the moving dawn light. The floral garlands on the blind, the soft green walls. The Chinese screen in front of the washstand, the small landscapes (watercolors painted by Uncle Ernst), the sunny yellow rag rug — everything is gray and moving, slowly, slowly. Father is sitting on a white chair with a high back. He has on a short nightshirt with a red border, is barefoot, his hands clasped. Pu thinks he is staring straight at him, but the eyes are unseeing and he can presumably see nothing but his own distress. The picture of his parents is indelible, despite the faint light. He remembers the picture. I can see it now or whenever I wish to. I can recall what was terrifying in their distance and immobility. The moment that was a mortal blow to Pu's well-controlled image of the world, in which even ghosts and punishments were evidence of a reality controlled by Pu. It fell apart or dissolved, leaving nothing. A king was dethroned and forced to leave his realm, and as the smallest and most wretched of all small and wretched people, he was forced to explore the country he had been robbed of, which to his terror lacked all boundaries. There was Mother sitting on the bed with her arms around her knees. There was Father sitting on a high-backed chair with his hands clasped and his gaze fixed on someone behind Pu's left ear. I do not remember what words were spoken. I remember the picture and the cold from the floor. I think I remember the tone of voice and the fine fragrance of Mother's flowers and Mother's soap. But I do not remember the words. They are invented, guessed, reconstructed sixty-four years after the actual moment.

"It's humiliating," says Father, drawing a deep breath.

"I told you you didn't have to come."

"I had to come for a very simple reason. I miss you and the children. I don't want to be alone. I've had enough of loneliness."

"Can't you try to be a little nice now, Erik? We're

so pleased to have you here — you must see that. Don't you?"

"Yes, I like to think that — but it's so humiliating. Then your mother trooping over with that fool Carl in tow. And she doesn't even ask whether it suits us."

"You're being really unfair now. Mama took the trouble to come here just to welcome you."

"She came to embarrass me. I know that base creature. What a triumph for her that we live here in this ramshackle hovel in this ramshackle landscape. Against *my* will. Against my *expressed* will."

"I didn't think servants of God were allowed to go around harboring so much hatred."

"I can't forgive a person who wants to destroy me."

"It's horrible to hear you."

"Oh, it's horrible, is it?"

"Yes, it's horrible. You sound just like your poor mother. You sound quite manic."

"I can't forgive a person who hates me just because I exist."

"You sound just like Mother Alma."

"We weren't so grand. No, that's it. We weren't so grand. That fits."

"You should hear your tone of voice."

"And you should hear yours when you say 'your poor mother.' "

"What *are* we doing, actually?"

"We couldn't go to the theater or travel to Italy and Mösseberg, and we couldn't afford to buy the latest novels."

"You really haven't anything to say about that. You've enjoyed my money just as much as the children and I have."

"Yes."

"You really mustn't talk like this."

"No."

"It's horrible when you go on like this."

"Yes, perhaps it is horrible. But I wasn't the one who simply had to live in Villagatan in that expensive apartment. We were perfectly all right in Skeppargatan."

"It got no sun, and the children were ill."

"So you usually say."

"Dr. Fürstenberg said —"

"I *know* what Dr. Fürstenberg said."

Mother is about to reply but stops and says nothing. She has started biting a nail and is furious. She says nothing and is recharging. Pu sees that Father has really given up, looking at his wife from the side as he goes to stand by the white desk, where he is now outlined against the white rectangle of the window blind. The silence festers, growing more and more terrifying. Father now has another voice:

"You say nothing."

"Do you think I ought to say something?"

"You can say what you like."

Father is afraid now, that's clear.

"So you mean I'm to say what I think," says Mother slowly.

Father says nothing and Mother says nothing. When Mother then speaks, her voice is as calm as snow. Pu feels his legs tingling and his stomach contracting, the tears rising into his eyes without his wanting to cry. He certainly does not want to hear what Mother has to say, but he can't move, his feet won't obey him, so he has to stay where he is and hear it.

Mother speaks. Her voice is calm, and she is looking at her forefinger and a torn-off piece of skin, which is bleeding slightly.

"You want to know what I think, do you? Well, I'm thinking about something that's been on my mind often over the last year. Or, if I'm to be completely honest, ever since Lillan was born."

"Perhaps I don't want to," says Father in a faint voice.

"But now *I* want to, and you can't stop me."

"I'd better go."

"Oh, well, don't mind me. But it might be good to talk honestly for once. Maybe it'll be good that we at last know where we stand with each other."

Mother looks at him and smiles faintly.

77

"For a long time I've thought of taking the children and leaving you for a while." Silence. The figure by the window is absolutely immobile. Mother turns her head and looks at him.

"I want to move to Upsala. There's a five-room apartment vacant at the top of the family property, and I can have it cheaply. It faces the courtyard and is sunny and quiet and recently renovated, with a bathroom and all conveniences. Dag and Pu will have a short way to school — it's just across the road. And Maj is sure to come with us to Upsala to look after Lillan. I thought of going back to work. I've written to Sister Elisabeth, and she says I am welcome. Then I will be nearer my brother Ernst and Mama and my best friends — without asking — without you — without — jealousy — and I'll be a little free — I — a little free —"

Some morning magpies can be heard in the birch tree beyond the blind, and it's slightly windy. The blind billows out. Father has lowered his head and is drawing with his finger on the desk blotter. Pu is rigid where he stands, frightened into deathly stillness.

"So you mean we should separate?"

"I didn't say that."

"You want us to separate, and you're thinking of leaving me?"

"Erik! Calm down now and try to listen to what —"

"You're leaving and taking the children with you."

"I have *never* mentioned divorce —"

"Is it Torsten who's filled you with these ideas?"

"No, it is not Torsten."

"But you've talked to him."

"Of course I've talked to him."

"You've talked about us to an outsider."

"He's our best friend, Erik! And he wishes us well."

"And of course your mother, and Ernst, of course your esteemed brother, and then Sister Elisabeth! Who *haven't* you talked to? Oh, the shame of it, the shame of it. You talk to everyone, but you don't talk to me. Because I think you rather like listening to strangers, but you don't want to listen to me."

Bitter irresolution. Pu still can't move. This is what he has feared most of all, the end with no mercy, punishment with no forgiveness; hurled into the darkness, he will land in a hole among sharp stones, and no one will look for him, no one will lift him out of the darkness.

"Well, now you know what I want to do," says Mother after a long silence. "You asked, and now you know."

"And if I hadn't asked?"

"I don't know, Erik. I don't know. I was waiting for an opportunity, but I was so uncertain."

"But now you're certain, I see."

"Can't you come and sit over here on the bed, Erik dear. You're so far away, and we must try to find a way out of this. Together. I don't want to hurt you."

"Oh, don't you?"

The pastor sounds more miserable than ironic. He sits down heavily at the foot of the bed, far out of his wife's reach. She tries to catch his wrist, but no.

"It's so difficult, Erik. I don't want to hurt you."

"So you said, yes."

"But when you come here, you get so restless and impatient. And at home we have so much to do. And you're always so worried about your sermons, we never have time to go away together, and if we do, then it has to be at my expense, and then you get so cross and contrary. Then I've my parish work and the housekeeping and the children, and sometimes it all gets terribly burdensome."

Father covers his face with his hands and snivels briefly. It all looks so strange and awful. Mother gets up on her knees to reach Father's cheek and stroke it, but he draws away and gets up.

"Are you going?" says Mother in dismay.

"I'm going for a walk. I need to."

"Now, in the middle of the night?"

"Yes, now, precisely."

"I'll come with you."

Mother at once gets off the bed and starts gathering her thick hair together. Her bare foot is small, high-arched and round-toed. "I'll come with you."

"No, thank you, Karin. I need to be alone."

"You can't just go like this."

"You can't tell me what to do."

"Don't go. It's even worse when you go."

Father has taken a few steps toward the door but stops and turns around. His voice is calm and unclouded.

"One thing you have to know, Karin," he says. "This is the last time you threaten me with leaving and taking the children with you. The *last time,* Karin! You and your mother. There must be a stop to these humiliations."

"This is no threat."

"All the worse. Then we know exactly how we stand."

"I suppose we do."

"I've always been alone. Now I really will be."

Father leaves, and Pu leaps silently in behind the nursery door as Father disappears down the creaking stairs, having snatched up his clothes from the chair by the closet on the way. Pu thinks of going in to his mother for consolation. He could say, for instance, that he couldn't sleep because he had a stomachache. That might work out well if Mother's in the right mood. But something tells him he is not likely to receive any consolation at this particular moment. He peeps at his mother. She is sitting upright in bed, her bare foot on the floor, sniffing dryly, running her hand over her cheek and forehead as if trying to remove an invisible cobweb. She sobs again twice, then draws a deep breath: yes, it's difficult.

The village roosters then start crowing, competing, one of them at Berglund's and the other at Törnqvist the gardener's.

Pu stands thinking for a long time, then he decides. Yes, he'll do that, that's exactly what he'll do. There's no point in going back to bed and pulling the covers over his head as if nothing had happened, now that his known world has collapsed before his very eyes and around his very ears. He patters into the nursery and quickly gets dressed: the faded shirt, the cut-off underpants, the short trousers and jersey, his sandals in his hand. Creeps down the stairs, avoiding the step that creaks. Exhaustion and agitation buzz in his stomach, and something horrible keeps squeezing his thin chest, but I won't cry, it's no use crying, there's no forgiveness any longer, there's no point in appealing with prayers and tears to God. God clearly doesn't care a shit for Pu. That's just what Pu has had an inkling of for a long time. His guardian angels have flapped away, and God has forgotten him. Perhaps he doesn't exist. The sky is white and cloudless, the sun thundering its vast wheel below Djurmo hill. The river was black and is now liquid silver, it's the next day, and he is warm under his jersey. A wind runs through the trees; the young swallows hurtle out in wobbly attempts to fly.

Pu sees his father immediately. He is sitting on the rickety summer bench below the veranda. He has put on his shirt with no collar and his shabby summer trousers. He still has his slippers on, and he's slung his leather jacket over his shoulders. He is smoking his pipe. There's dew in the grass, and Pu gets his feet wet. He goes up to the bench and sits down.

Father looks down at Pu in surprise.

"You up at this hour?"

"I was going for a little walk in the forest."

"Oh, yes. May I ask why?"

"I was going to see if I could see a ghost."

"You were going to see a ghost?"

"A specter."

"Where were you going to find him?"

"At the suicide spot."

"The watchmaker?"

"I'm a Sunday's child."

"Do you really believe in ghosts?"

"Lalla and Maj say they exist."

"Well, in that case."

The conversation comes to an end. Father's pipe

gurgles. When it goes out, he lights it again, and Pu draws in the smell he likes.

"Pipe smoke's good against the midges," says Father.

"There are quite a lot of them for so early in the year," says Pu politely.

Then it is quiet again. The sun wells up on the mountain ridge, already white and blazing. Pu closes his eyes, now smarting behind his eyelids.

"Would you like to come with me to Grånäs? We'd take the train to Djurås, then cycle about six miles."

Father turns his big face to Pu and looks at him with a blue gaze, then takes his pipe out of his mouth and asks again. Pu says nothing, now faced with an insoluble dilemma. Father is miserable and asking Pu to go with him. He can't say no.

"I was going to play trains and put down tracks all the way from the privy, where I was going to make the station, down to the birch, where I'd put the switches and the turntable. Jonte was going to come and play with me. He told me he was going to."

"I see. You don't have to decide at once. Think about it."

Father smiles kindly and knocks his pipe out against the bench. Pu catches a ladybug on his finger. The weight on his chest is still there.

"We'd go by that little freight train that leaves from

Dufnäs at nine on Sundays with nothing but lumber cars and one old coach. Then we can buy some Pommac to go with our box lunch."

They are sitting together, with a gap of six feet. The dew is still evaporating, a streak of mist lying over the river; it's going to be a hot day.

I'll now recount a flashback into the future. The year is nineteen hundred and sixty-eight. Father is eighty-two and recently a widower. He lives in a five-room apartment in Östermalm, Stockholm. Sister Edit looks after the household. She is a deaconess and is fifty-eight, a handsome lady of healthy femininity and warm dark-brown eyes beneath long eyelashes. Her mouth is large and often laughing, her hands are broad and dry. Sister Edit was one of Father's very first confirmation candidates and became a friend of the family. She speaks an articulate Hälsinge dialect.

Father was severely disabled by his hereditary muscular dystrophy. He wore orthopedic boots and used a stick, his long, shapely hands partially atrophied. Between Father and Sister Edit, a wordless but affectionate relationship prevailed. They obviously got on very well together.

I was on my way up Grevturegatan. It was early spring, with sleet and strong indirect light above the melting snowdrifts and the icy, poorly sanded pavement. For a year now, Father and I had lived in outward reconciliation and courteous mutual understanding. By that I do not mean we had delved into the complications of the past, the distancing, the misunderstandings and hatred. We never mentioned our differences, which had stretched over a generation. But our distress had superficially evaporated. To me, my hatred of my father was a strange illness that had once, an eternity ago, afflicted someone else — not me. Nowadays I helped Father with his finances and some administration — nothing burdensome. I visited him and Sister Edit every Saturday afternoon and stayed for a few hours. It is about one of those visits I wish to tell.

I took the elevator, and with creaking Östermalm dignity, it carried me up to the top floor of the apartment house. I rang two short signals on the bell, and Sister Edit at once came and opened the door. She put her forefinger to her lips and whispered that we should be rather quiet: Father had extended his midday rest by an hour. He had had a bad night, with pain in his hip and back. I whispered that in that case, Sister Edit and I could talk a little business. Sister Edit thought it a good idea. She asked me if I would like some coffee or perhaps tea. She had just made scones. No, thank you; I've just come from a long lunch with some Scandinavian theater managers, no thank you. I stripped off my overcoat, removed my wet winter shoes, was lent a pair of Father's slippers, and we sat down in Sister Edit's room. It faced the street, and though not particularly large, it was cozily furnished: light wallpaper, lovely gentle pictures and reproductions, airy curtains, a well-stocked bookcase, a small two-seater sofa and an armchair, an elaborately ornate clock. The bedspread was a wide crocheted blanket in yellow tones. A white desk and two chairs stood over by the window. We sat down at the desk. Edit took out a file and, largely for the sake of order, showed me some bills that had been paid, a cash withdrawal receipt, and a letter from the landlord saying the rent was to rise from the first of July. Edit read out the letter and sighed.

"You see, Ingmar, the worst of it is that Erik keeps worrying about his finances. It doesn't make any difference that I say we're perfectly all right."

"I'll speak to Father."

"Please, Ingmar, could you at the same time tell Erik that I have no intention of leaving him and, most of all, that you're not thinking of putting him in a geriatric ward."

"Oh, I see. Is that what he says?"

"He thinks we want to get hold of the apartment."

"The apartment?"

"He sometimes says that you and I want to get hold of the apartment. And that it's only a matter of time

87

before we make him go into a geriatric ward. Then he gets terribly distressed, and nothing helps."

"And how are you, Edit?"

"I'm almost always perfectly well. No, what worries me is that your father is so miserable. And he's so isolated. He's tormented, you see, Ingmar, and I stand beside him unable to do anything. And then there's this business with Death."

"Death?"

"To be honest, Ingmar, I think your father is afraid of Death and all that. He doesn't say so directly, but I know the way Erik thinks. As he doesn't want to show he's worried, he's lonely in that quarter too. And gets impatient and quarrels about silly little things. No, I don't mind. He can nag and quarrel if he likes. He doesn't mean any harm. And sometimes when he's been particularly troublesome over some minor nonsense, he goes out and comes back with flowers for me. So when it comes down to it, we're fairly all right together. But this business about Death is probably really difficult. I can't help him with it, and I don't understand his anguish. He's a priest, after all, and ought to put his trust in the mercy of Christ. But I think he's lost his faith. Poor Erik, who's been such a prop to so many people — me too; not least me. His faith was so pure and strong — well, you know that, Ingmar: sometimes he seemed to be translucent from his conviction. The year after Karin's death, we talked often to each other about the miracle of reunion. He was convinced he and Karin would meet in another country, cleansed and transfigured. There was real joy in our talks, and I thought that God is merciful to allow an old person to remain so certain of his resurrection. I don't know, Ingmar. Now I'm crying a little, but that's nothing to worry about. I just feel so sorry for your father. He's such a good man. Why should he be devastated in this way while he's alive? It's cruel, and I don't understand the meaning of it. I'm so fond of him, and I really do want to do everything I can to give him a little peace and joy in his last years."

Sister Edit blew her nose with a little trumpeting sound. She was definitely one of those people who become more beautiful when they cry. She wiped her nose and the tears from her eyes. Then she laughed.

"I really am awful, me too, crying like a young girl. Are you sure you wouldn't like a cup of tea, Ingmar? It's already four o'clock. I wonder whether I should go and wake your father up after all. Are you in a hurry, Ingmar? Wait a moment, I think I can hear him. Yes, here he comes. While I remember, I've received a copy of that transfer you arranged. You'd better take it with you."

Sister Edit got up with a briskness that comes from steadiness of soul and obvious delight. Father's footsteps were stumping along the corridor. He was moving heavily in his orthopedic boots, and his stick thumped. He knocked. Edit called, Come in, and Father opened the door. I was just going to get up to go over to him but stopped. He had remained in the doorway and was looking at us with an absent gaze. His thin hair was ruffled and one ear dark red. He was wearing his ancient dark-green dressing gown that smelled of cigars, his blue-veined hand clutching his stick hard.

"I just wanted to know if Karin was back yet," he mumbled, looking at Edit and me without recognizing us.

"Has Karin come back yet?"

At that moment his face changed.

He realized with painful vehemence where he was and what the reality was. Karin was dead, and he had made a fool of himself. He smiled a dreadful smile and apologized. I'm sorry, I'm clearly not quite awake. Good day, my son. I suppose you can come in to me for a little while?

Then he turned and stumped back through the dark corridor to his room. Edit remained standing, the document folder in her hand.

"It's nothing. You needn't be afraid, Ingmar. Erik sometimes thinks Karin is somewhere near. He gets so upset when he finds he's mistaken. Partly that Karin's dead and, perhaps worst of all, that he's made a fool of himself. I'll go in to him now. You can come in a quarter of an hour."

Father leans over toward Pu. I think you're about to fall asleep. Won't you go back to bed? It's only five o'clock. You can sleep for at least three hours. Pu shakes his head but says nothing: No, thank you; I want to sit here and watch the sun. I want to sit here with Father. I want to keep watch on my father so that he doesn't whisk away just like that. I'm sleepy but miserable. No, I've no intention of going back to bed and smelling Dag's morning farts and noisy shitting. I always lose when we compete, anyhow. Pu yawns hugely and falls asleep as abruptly as a candle goes out in a draft. He sits with his chin on his chest and his hands open against the slats of the bench. The thin hair at the nape of his head is sticking straight out, and the sun shines on his cheek. Father sits without moving, looking at his son. His pipe has gone out.

In his dream, Pu is walking through a forest that he both knows and doesn't know. The stream gurgles and splashes. Flashes of sunlight move above his head, and where he's walking it is shady but close. He keeps moving on without wanting to. Then he stops and looks around. This is undoubtedly the suicide place, and he needn't wait for long. The stream is gurgling, but otherwise it's quiet, the ants in the anthill and on the path darting about soundlessly. There's no longer rising sunlight here, only gray shadow and an oppressive heat, though it's chilly. Pu is cold and hunches down. Someone is moving about on the other side of the double pine: he can see the watchmaker's back. He's standing there with his shoulders hunched up and his thin hair falling over his dirty collar. He turns around and looks at Pu with empty bulging eyes and no pupils, his mouth hanging open and black with dried blood, his eyebrows so light they hardly exist, his forehead far too high and gray, covered with spots. I don't want this. It's not true. I don't want to be part of this; I can't cry and I can't run away. The watchmaker has taken away all my strength in order to reveal himself — I've heard that somewhere, perhaps it was Lalla: ghosts use people's strength to be able to reveal themselves, that's why you go all stiff — now I'm caught; it feels as if I'm suffocating. Pu says something through chattering teeth: I'm very sorry, I didn't really want to come, but now I'm here, anyhow. There's something wrong with me, doing this. I can't remember how I got here — suppose I'm dreaming. Suppose things are so horribly arranged that I'm dreaming and asleep and will never wake up again.

Pu's anxiety rises like a hot ray, his whole body filled with uncontrollable pain. The watchmaker stands facing Pu. A green shimmer attenuates the ghost. The figure sways and wafts about, although there's no wind. So, Sunday's child and the Feast of the Transfiguration. Now it's a question of asking. And Pu asks once and, when he gets no answer, once again: *When shall I die?* The watchmaker thinks, and then Pu seems to hear a whisper, which is unclear and blurred because of that bloodstained mouth and those stiff lips: Always. The answer to the question is: *always.*

A faint puff of wind through the forest, a jackdaw calling somewhere. The watchmaker sways in the wind, and his head comes away from his neck and shoulders, approaches, and Pu wonders if his last moment has arrived. He wonders if the head will fasten its teeth into his bare arms or his knee. The face has a dissolved but evil expression. But the wind turns and disperses the face, the eyes hanging below the pine branches; they go out, the whole ghost goes out, his arms sucked down into the ground, first the right arm, the hands opening and the black nails falling like rotten apples. The whole watchmaker folds, and Pu sees the red wound from the rope and bits of bone sticking out of the neck. Everything suddenly goes quickly, then he's gone, now there's nothing left but the smell, the smell of mold like under the linoleum in the nursery.

With a great effort, he steps out of his dream and opens his eyes wide so as not to be deceived back into that other world. Father is filling his pipe. Marianne is beside him. She has just come up from the river and has been swimming. Her short, dark hair lies close to her head, and her face is turned to the sun. She is wearing long trousers and a thin top, her breasts outlined through the material. She is barefoot. Father says something about it's soon being seven o'clock and time to shave. Marianne tells him it was lovely swimming down there by the raft, though the logs have broken through the barriers and piled up in the mud on the shore. But it was lovely, because I was alone and could bathe naked. It was awfully cold, no more than fifty-five degrees, I would think, but they say the river is particularly cold this year. Thank goodness for the archipelago, says Father, lighting his pipe. You don't drown in the shore mud there.

"Is Pu going with you to Grånäs?"

"I don't know. I asked him, but he didn't seem all that enthusiastic."

"*I* could go with you," suggests Marianne.

"Aren't you staying home to keep Karin company?"

"I'd like a bicycle ride."

"Uhuh." Father nods gravely.

"With you."

"Pu'll probably be pleased not to have to go."

"All three of us could go."

"He was going to build a railway line between the privy and the sandpile. And Jonte was going to come and help."

"So, what do you think? What would you like?" says Marianne.

"Well, it'd be nice," says Father hesitantly.

Pu stretches and yawns loudly.

"I'll go with you to Grånäs," he says firmly.

Father and Marianne look at Pu with some surprise: Oh, so you're awake — well, I'll be darned. Yes, says Pu, I'm awake, but now I'm going back to bed to finish sleeping. But I'll go with you to Grånäs. He gets up and, with his eyes half closed, trots around the corner of the house, up the stairs, and into the nursery, takes off his clothes and sandals, and tumbles into his complaining bed, burying his head in the pillow. He's sound asleep before he falls asleep.

It's ten to eight, and Maj is shaking him roughly. Dag is already dressed. He has fetched the carafe from Mother's room and is pouring water over his brother. Stop it, shrieks Pu, and Dag laughs. Goddamn shit in hell, yells Pu, defending himself. Dag retreats and throws a sandal at his brother. Maj intervenes before the conflict has escalated into fratricide.

Pu has to subject himself to yet further indignities. Maj makes him clean his teeth, wash his ears, and have his nails cleaned and cut. He also has to have clean clothes: a clean undershirt that tickles, a clean shirt, which is too long, and clean underpants: God, you always smell of piss, says brother Dag unkindly. Don't you undo your fly when you pee? His Sunday trousers are taken out of the closet, dark-blue short trousers with stiff creases and idiotic suspenders. Pu protests, but Maj is relentless and prepared to resort to force if necessary. Blow your nose! she orders, holding a clean handkerchief against Pu's nose. I don't understand why you've got so many boogers.

"That's because he's always got his finger up his nose," says Dag, who has been witnessing the humiliating dressing. "If you find anything, we'll share it, eh?" Dag thunders down the stairs. Pu sits on the bed, a leaden sleepiness falling over him. Maj comes out of the closet. What's the matter? she says quite kindly. I feel sick, mumbles Pu. You'll feel better when you've had something to eat. Come on now, Pu.

His intestines are rolling around and in turmoil, a hard lump of shit pressing against his asshole, wanting out. I must go and shit, says Pu unhappily; it's absolutely necessary. That can wait until after breakfast, Maj decides. It can't, I must shit *now*, he whispers, almost in tears. Hurry on out, then — run! I must *shit now*, repeats Pu. Use the pail, says Maj, kicking out the enamel pail, which is half full of dirty washing water. She helps Pu with his suspenders and pulls down his trousers and underpants. It's a last-minute operation. I've got a terrible goddamn awful bellyache, complains Pu. Maj sits on the bed and holds his hand. It'll be all right in a minute, she says kindly.

Märta calls from the stairs. Is Pu there? Time for breakfast. Is Pu there? Hey, Maj! Pu's got a stomachache, calls Maj, still holding his hand. We'll be down when we'll be down.

Pu has a stomachache, Märta passes on to Mother. Both of them are on the stairs. A bad one? Mother asks. No, it's all right; we'll soon be ready, Maj says soothingly. Talk and noise come from the dining room, the clatter of plates and cutlery. Well, then come as soon as you can, says Mother, on her way down.

Pu's forehead is sweaty, and he is pale beneath his suntan. His eyes have crept far back into his head, and his lips are dry. Maj strokes his forehead. You haven't got a temperature, anyhow. There's nothing really wrong with you, is there? Heavens, what a smell! Did you eat something silly, maybe? Pu shakes his head, and another pressing wave runs through his body. Damned hellish damned shit, he says, leaning forward. Damn. Hell. Dammit to hell. Is there something troubling you? says Maj. What? says Pu, his mouth open. For a moment the pain abates. Are you *unhappy* about something? No. Is something *worrying* you? No.

The attack has abated; color returns to Pu's cheeks, and he begins to breathe normally. I must have something to wipe myself with. We can take some paper from your sketchbooks, Maj suggests. But that's probably too thick. What about this red tissue paper? No, for Christ's sake, says Pu. That's Dag's. He uses it for his model airplane. If we take that, he'll kill me. I know, says Maj decisively. We'll use your washcloth. It can't be helped. I'll wash it afterward. Up with your backside, Pu. There we are. That was good, wasn't it?

At breakfast the scenario is much the same as at dinner. The only difference is a certain formality in clothing, as it's Sunday, Sunday the twenty-ninth of July and, as has been mentioned, the Feast of the Transfiguration. There isn't a white cloth on the table, either, but yellow patterned oilcloth. A copper vessel full of meadow flowers stands enthroned below the ceiling light.

Sunday morning at about eight. Royal customs reign in the Bergman family. On weekdays, breakfast is at half past seven, and on Sundays, half an hour later as a sloppy concession to Mother's liking to sleep in.

On the other hand, Father is morning cheerful. He's already had a swim in the river, shaved, and read through his sermon. He is almost exhilarated by the coming excursion. Pu has been given a plate of warm gruel instead of the usual oatmeal. Fragrant mild gruel and a piece of white bread with cheese. Lalla has prepared it with her own hands. No one dares oppose her, although both parental authorities and one or two of the others consider that Pu's gruel is nonsense and that all forms of nonsense are the originators and encouragers of vices. But no one dares protest Lalla's gruel, neither Mother nor Father nor anyone else. Pu shovels it in and is quite content but silent. The pain has sunk away and left a pleasing numbness, Lalla's gruel filling the hollow and warming him inside. Stomachaches make you very cold.

The door into the hall and the door to the outer porch are both open. The sandy yard is sparkling in the bright sunlight.

"It's going to be hot today," says Mother. "I wonder if there'll be a thunderstorm." Everyone comments on the prospect of thunder. Aunt Emma is convinced. She's felt it in her knees for several days. Lalla says the soured milk in the cellar has cracked and split, the first time that summer. Märta maintains that it's difficult to breathe. She is red under her eyes, and her upper lip is sweaty, so she's probably got a fever. Father says brightly that a little bad weather won't do any harm and the farmers need the rain. If it rains, the fish'll rise well, says Dag, grinning maliciously. Will my poor little brother be able to stand the rain? And he's so dreadfully scared of thunder.

And so the talk goes on. "While we talk, life passes," says Chekhov, and perhaps that's so. The doorway to the stairs is suddenly filled with a portly, somewhat unsteady figure. It is Uncle Carl, standing there with a little suitcase in his hand. He smiles with embarrassment. Well, well, hello, Carl, cries Father. Come on in and have a bite and a quick nip. My word, you look as if you've sold the butter and lost the money! Come on in and sit down, Carl dear, says Mother. Her voice is not quite so heartfelt as Father's. Has something happened, that you've got a suitcase? Shall I set a place? says Märta, half getting up. No, no, thank you, please don't trouble, mumbles Carl, wiping sweat away with a grubby handkerchief. Maybe I could just sit down for a moment?

Without waiting for a reply, he trots around the

room, greeting everyone and bowing in all directions, then sinks down on the sofa by the window. Father has fetched a glass and a bottle from the sideboard. Help yourself, brother. Carl empties the glass in one fell swoop, his pince-nez misting over. Thank you, Erik, thanks very much. You're truly a Christian man, who looks with mercy on the most wretched of the wretched.

"Has something happened?" Mother repeats her question and looks sternly at her half brother. Carl polishes his pince-nez and appears anxious. He laughs with embarrassment.

"I don't know about happened. Things happen all the time, don't they? A time to cast away stones and a time to gather stones together, as the Scriptures say."

"But you're clearly going away?" says Father, just as cheerfully as before.

"I'm thinking of moving, anyhow."

"Are you going to move? Where will *you* move to? If I may ask." There's a slight chill in Mother's voice.

"I'm not quite sure. But the important thing is that I maintain my human dignity."

"What has happened?" A third time. Mother is now more worried than stern. Carl puts his glasses back on and squirms. They are all regarding him with interest.

101

"I think I'll have a talk with Erik. What I have to say is scarcely suitable for babes and sucklings."

"Then you must stay here for the day and have a rest, and we'll have a talk this evening," says Father quickly, without consulting Mother even with a glance. "I'm in a slight hurry at the moment. Pu and I are to cycle to Grånäs and preach. But we're sure to be back in time for dinner at Våroms."

Uncle Carl's blue eyes fill with tears. He keeps nodding repeatedly to confirm the agreement.

"You're a good man, Erik!"

Mother makes a sign, and everyone gets up and says grace: For what we have just received may the Lord make us truly thankful. Amen. We're leaving at exactly quarter to nine, commands Father, looking at his gold watch, which is fastened with a gold chain and is wound with a tiny key. Then he turns to Uncle Carl: If you care to stay a night or two, I'm sure that will be all right. We'll all squash up a bit. Won't we, Karin? But Mother doesn't reply, just shakes her head and goes out into the kitchen with the porridge tureen.

"Would you like to earn twenty-five öre?" says Dag, grinning in a friendly way at Pu. He has his right hand behind his back. They are in back of the kitchen steps, where Pu has just peed, although that's forbidden.

"Of course I'd like to earn twenty-five öre."

"Good. I'll put the twenty-five öre there." Dag puts the coin down on the step. He seems mysteriously excited.

"What do I do now?"

"Eat this worm."

"What?"

"Close your mouth and don't look so stupid."

"You want me to eat that *worm?*"

Dag is holding the wriggling angleworm in front of Pu's nose.

"*Never!* I'll never eat a worm."

"But what if you get fifty öre?"

"No. *Never!*"

"Seventy-five öre, then, Pu? That's a hell of a lot of money."

Sudd the poodle has come out on the steps and is licking his lips after breakfast. He wags his tail fawningly at his god and looks at Pu, his antagonist, with derisive eyes.

"Why do you want me to eat that worm? It's disgusting."

"I've been given the assignment by the other boys to test your courage."

"What? What do you mean?"

"Well, if you're brave, then you can join our secret society and *also* earn seventy-five öre."

"How about a krona?"

"Don't be crazy. A krona! You'll have to eat up one of Aunt Emma's hunks of shit for that."

"Have you *got* seventy-five öre?" says Pu suspiciously.

"Here, look. Three shiny twenty-five öres. Here you are. And here's the worm. Well?"

"I could eat half."

"What kind of balls is *that*! You have to eat the whole worm or nothing. Just as I suspected. You're a cowardly shit, who'll never be allowed to join our society — what do *you* say, Sudd?"

Dag turns to Sudd, who opens his mouth and lets his long tongue slide out. It's quite obvious that Sudd is grinning.

"Gimme the damned worm," says Pu, raging with anger and the desire for money. He puts the whole worm into his mouth and munches and munches and munches. His eyes filling with tears, he goes on munching. The worm wriggles and twists under his tongue, a bit tries to escape out of the corner of his mouth, but Pu pokes it back. Then he swallows and swallows. His stomach threatens to revolt, but he subdues it.

"Now I've eaten the worm," says Pu.

"Open your mouth, so I can check."

Pu opens his mouth and his brother checks, looking for a long time. Then he says Pu can shut his

104

mouth again so the worm doesn't pop out. After that he gathers up his three twenty-five öres and calls Sudd.

"What the hell!" wails Pu.

Dag turns around and looks resignedly at his brother. "The boys and I thought we'd see just how stupid you are. If you're so damned stupid that you eat a worm for seventy-five öre, then you're far too stupid to join our society and *absolutely* too stupid to deserve seventy-five öre."

Pu flies at his brother but receives a goodly blow in the solar plexus, while at the same time Sudd bites his leg. Pu is gasping for breath and remains seated on the kitchen steps. Dag and Sudd leave, chatting happily. They meet Marianne in the yard. Pu can't hear what they're saying, but he reckons they're planning something pleasant. He fights down the worm and wonders whether he ought to be sick, perhaps put his fingers down his throat, but he hesitates. He's not going to give his brother that satisfaction. For a moment, life isn't worth a piss. *A worm in your stomach and a church service in Grånäs!* Pu collapses on the steps. No one in the entire world has such a damned awful time of it as he does.

Father is in the arbor with Uncle Carl, smoking his post-breakfast pipe, and Uncle Carl has been offered a cigar as well as supplied with another nip.

He is talking without stopping, and Father is smiling encouragingly. Why is Father suddenly being so friendly with Uncle Carl? Then Father looks at his watch and presumably says he and Pu must be going now if they're not to be late for the train, which is usually particularly punctual on Sundays. He gets up and pats Carl on the arm. Mother comes out onto the front steps, calling for Pu. She has Father's green suitcase in her hand. Dag wheels out the bicycle, and the case is fastened on the back carrier. The front carrier is reserved for Pu. Marianne puts a little bunch of harebells in Father's lapel. Märta comes running out with her box camera. She enjoys taking photographs. Aunt Emma has been to the privy after breakfast and is cautiously waddling down the path. She has a copy of *Gefle Dagblad* under her arm. Lalla comes out of the kitchen with the box lunch, and after some palaver it is squashed into the case, along with Father's starched collar, a clean white shirt, his cassock, and the sermon itself. What if the bottle of milk breaks and ruins the cassock and the sermon? At first the plan is to put the bottle of milk at the bottom and the clothes on top, but then the milk is omitted. There'll be coffee at the pastor's, and Father has promised Pu a Pommac, which is to be purchased from the village store on the way home.

Now Märta is ready to take a photograph and

wants Mother to be in the picture and appear to be saying good-bye to Father, but Mother resists: No, thank you; the travelers will have to pose alone. In the end, a photograph is arrived at: Father standing rather stiffly, holding the steeply raised handlebars. He is wearing a light jacket and a hat. He has put on his black preacher's trousers, for there was no room for them in the case, and has fastened the bottoms with bicycle clips. A white collarless shirt and boots complete the outfit. Pu has on the clothing previously described, plus a white linen hat that is a trifle too large and rests on his protruding ears. His face is in shadow. He is already perched up on the front carrier, holding out his long legs.

Everyone is talking at once and wishing them a good trip, Mother saying that Grandmother is postponing dinner a whole hour and they simply *mustn't* be late. Aunt Emma says there's going to be a thunderstorm, there's sure to be a thunderstorm.

Far away, beyond the heath, above the distant mountains, there's a black edge of cloud and some white clouds stretching their thin fingers toward the top of the sky. The harbinger of the storm, says Aunt Emma. Mother gives Pu a kiss and says at least twice that he must be careful not to get his foot caught in the spokes of the front wheel. Uncle Carl waves his cigar from the arbor. "Good soul-fishing, esteemed brother!" Dag is hanging on to Marianne, and Sudd is hanging on to Dag. Maj is making the bed in Mother's room upstairs. She draws aside the lace curtain over the unopenable window and calls to Pu and waves. Pu waves feebly back. Maj's Sunday summer dress has a square neck, and when she leans forward Pu can see her breasts. Her reddish hair is newly washed, rebelling against its braid, and is standing like fire around her kind freckled face.

THE JOURNEY STARTS with a breakneck run downhill. Father is an accomplished but daredevil cyclist. The hill from the Dahlberg dwelling is both full of holes and stony; it is also narrow and, as mentioned, steep.

When they reach the road, Father begins to pedal. Heavens, it's hot, he says, taking off his hat and handing it to Pu. Careful with my hat.

The freight train is already in the station, and the little shunter is busy shunting: heavily laden lumber cars are to go to the sawmill at Gimån, empty cars taken to Insjön lumberyard, and three cars loaded with sweet-smelling, newly sawed planks are to wait at Dufnäs station for transportation to the building site of the new Good Templar Hall. The brakemen have come down from their cramped boxes and are strolling along the platform, one drinking out of a bottle of beer and eating a sandwich, another smoking his pipe; the stationman rushes between the south switches over by the bridge; the little engine backs and puffs as two men struggle with the couplings, and the buffers and the heavy hooks clang. The sun is directly above the river bend.

Father and Pu go into the office to see Uncle Ericsson. Ah, so the Pastor's off away this Sunday, is he, and his son's going too? I'm preaching in Grånäs, says Father. That means the train to Djurås and then on by bicycle, I suppose? says Uncle Ericsson, taking a little brown cardboard ticket out of the ticket cupboard. He stamps it in his stamping machine. Do I have to register the bicycle? says Father. No, you can take it into the compartment. No one gets on until Leksand on a Sunday.

Mrs. Ericsson comes down from the floor above. Her neck is badly misshapen by a goiter, and her eyes almost bulge out of their sockets. She smiles toothlessly and broadly. She has a brimming cup of coffee in her hand. I thought perhaps the pastor might like a cup, she says in her Orsa accent. And perhaps little Pu would like a sweet? She takes a sticky paper twist out of her apron pocket and offers him a homemade bull's-eye. Pu bows and thanks her. And how are you, Mrs. Ericsson? says Father, looking straight into Mrs. Ericsson's wide-open eyes. Well, not so good, Pastor. I went to the hospital in Falun last week because I'm beginning to get breathless at night. The doctor says I ought to have an operation. He wants to take away a bit of the thyroid gland, but I don't know, though choking is horrid, but I take iodized salt every day, though it doesn't help much. I just get worse. And I look so awful. Last summer the goiter didn't show. It's got this bad this winter. It all started when I had tuberculosis and I lost — well, you know, Pastor. No, things aren't too good, and it gets suffocating up there in our rooms and we get the evening sun in our bedroom, so some nights I move to a mattress down in the waiting room. That faces north, so there's always a bit of cool there. But the railway inspector was here and saw the mattress, and he said I was not allowed to be in the waiting room, that it was forbidden, but then Ericsson said he didn't care a goddamn fig about that and said the inspector could sue us if he liked, and then he took off.

Pu has climbed up to the window facing the station area, more interested in the little shunting engine's efforts than in Mrs. Ericsson's goiter. He is sucking on his bull's-eye and watching the two lumber flatcars. They've been given a little shove by the shunter and are rolling obligingly to the track nearest the station house. One of the men has put out a brake block, and the heavy cars stop good-naturedly, jerking back and forth a little as if they were alive.

"They're ready now!" cries Pu, and climbs down

from the window. "They're ready!" Pu wants to be off; what is after all a rather brief train journey is causing some excitement. Well, we'll be off, then, Pastor. Uncle Ericsson fetches his uniform cap and the red flag fastened to a round green platter. If you signal with the green plate, that means "ready for departure." Father drinks up his coffee, right down to the grounds, says thank you, and shakes Mrs. Ericsson by the hand. I'll speak to a friend of mine named Professor Forsell about your illness, Mrs. Ericsson. Maybe he has a solution.

"Thank you, thank you, but please don't go to any trouble, Pastor."

One of the brakemen helps lift the bicycle and suitcase into the small coach at the back of the freight train. It's a very elderly coach, greenish-gray and with doors at the sides. The inside is Spartan: twelve short wooden seats placed opposite each other, six on each side of a middle aisle, a spittoon by every other bench. The floor is covered with worn brown-patterned linoleum, and at one end towers an iron stove. The little windows are down on this summer morning. Two glass globes in the ceiling contain gaslights, and the whole carriage smells of varnished wood and iron.

Pu hangs out the window, still excited. He's to go by train, and in few moments Uncle Ericsson will give the signal, the engine will puff out a black cloud, and the cars will roll along the rails. Father has found a newspaper, the *Borlänge Post,* and is studying the Public Notices: In Grånäs Church in Gagnef parish tomorrow, Sunday, at 11 A.M., Pastor Erik Bergman from Stockholm will be preaching. Holy Communion will be held at the service.

But the train does not leave. Pu leans dangerously far out of the window to find out why. Uncle Ericsson is reading some papers, and the stationman is explaining and pointing. The engine pants and sighs, as if deploring the troublesome heat and the uphill slopes to come. Mrs. Ericsson's misshapen face can be glimpsed behind the curtains upstairs in the station house.

Then they hear voices, and Pu turns and looks the other way. Marianne, Dag, and Uncle Carl are approaching at a rapid pace, carrying fishing rods, and Dag has the bait tin with its perforated lid and its handle. Uncle Carl has a knapsack on his back with their box lunches.

"Hello!" cries Marianne. "Haven't you gone yet?"

"Where are you off to?" says Father, coming up beside Pu in the narrow window.

"We're going fishing at Kallbäcken," trumpets Uncle Carl. "Ma was on her way, so my sister Karin arranged a little outing. She thought it'd be better to talk on her own with Ma. And *I* had no objections to *that.*"

At last the little freight train starts moving, with mighty screeches and energetic puffs of smoke. Everyone waves. For a moment, Pu sees Marianne putting her arm around Dag's shoulders. He smiles with delight and waves enthusiastically to his brother. They disappear out of sight, and the wind and the acrid coal smoke assail Pu's face.

The engine hoots on the bend below the mountain, the coach rocks, the wheels click over the rail joints. Then they leave the river and dive into the forest. The engine chugs heavily uphill, the little wooden coach clattering and shaking. Sit down on the bench, says Father. You mustn't hang out of the window. It can be dangerous. Father takes hold of Pu's waistband and pulls him down. Father and son sit opposite each other, Father still reading his paper.

"Father?"

"Yes." Father puts his paper down.

"What's *history*?"

"It's the story of the past."

"Then is Grandfather's death history?"

"There are different kinds of history. There's the major history of wars and kings and whole peoples, and then there's the minor history, the history of family life. So in that way, you could say Grandfather's death is also history."

Father is leaning forward with his elbows on his thighs, his hands clasped, looking attentively at his son. Whenever Father talks to anyone, whoever it may be, he looks the person straight in the eye and listens properly.

"You don't like being with us at Dufnäs, do you, Father?"

"I'm not all that keen on Dufnäs, that's all. I like Mother and my children, but not Dufnäs."

"Why don't you like Dufnäs?"

"I feel shut in, if you see what I mean."

"No."

"I can't decide things for myself."

"Does Grandmother decide?"

"You could perhaps say that."

"So that's why you hate Grandmother?"

"Hate?"

The corners of Father's mouth twitch slightly, and he looks down at his clasped hands.

"Dag says you and Grandmother hate each other."

"Grandmother and I think differently in lots of ways. Yes, nearly all ways. So we get angry. You must see that."

"Yes."

"Sometimes it gets awfully difficult. Especially in

115

the summers. When we live so close to each other, troubles easily come about. It's easier in the winter, when Grandmother's in Upsala and we're in Stockholm."

"I like Grandmother."

"You must go on liking your grandmother. Grandmother likes you, and you like Grandmother. That's just as it should be."

"Would you be pleased if Grandmother died?"

"Now listen! Why should I be pleased? First of all, I know you and Mother and Dag and lots of other people would be sad, and secondly, one doesn't think that sort of thing."

Pu considers it. This is both difficult and important. Also, it's not often that Father has time to talk. He must make the most of it.

"Oh, yes," says Pu sorrowfully. "But I wish that lots of people would be dead and become history! Aunt Emma and Dag — "

"That's quite another matter," Father interrupts. "You're not thinking about what death is. So you just throw out wishes like that without really meaning anything."

"Sometimes I think Mother's dead, and then I'm miserable."

"Perhaps you sometimes wish your father were dead? When you're angry, for instance."

Father is smiling with his mouth and his eyes, his voice harmless. This is a *real* conversation, thinks Pu. Pu usually carries on conversations or "discussions" with Grandmother in the evenings in Upsala when he goes to see her over the Christmas holiday. Mother and Father never have time for discussions.

"I've never wished you were dead, Father," lies Pu, with an honest expression.

Father pats Pu on the cheek, his smile still there.

"You must forgive me, Pu, but sometimes you do ask really silly questions."

Pu nods brightly and responds to Father's smile.

The train slows down with considerable noise, rattling, clanking, and clattering, the forest opening up under the hills and a few farms appearing on the steep slopes. Father taps Pu's knee. We're there now. Don't forget your hat, and you look after mine.

The train stops at Djurås, where the road crosses the railway line, no sidings, no signals, nothing but a leaking wooden platform, a small cottage. The crossing keeper, a fat woman, limps out of the cottage, turning sideways to get through the door. She knows the pastor, says good day, then helps him get down the bicycle and case. The heat is like a wall, and a cow is lowing down the slope. The engineer looks out of his cab and vaguely salutes father and son. The keeper gives the all-clear sign, and the train glides away down

117

the slope toward Sifferbo, with no smoke, puffing, or clanking.

"Would the pastor like a cup of coffee?" says the fat woman.

"No, thank you, Mrs. Brogren. We're late already."

"It's dreadful that I never get to church, but Olsson's in the hospital and I'm on my own weekdays as well as Sundays. Wouldn't your son like a little juice?"

"No, thank you," says Pu politely.

"Then I wish you all the best on your trip."

"Thank you, Mrs. Brogren, and regards to Mr. Olsson."

"Pastor, do you think God punishes us?"

"Why should God punish anyone?"

"I mean because Olsson and I live in sin, as the mission director says. He was here last month making a fuss, and the next day Olsson trod on a rusty nail so he got blood poisoning and had to go to the hospital. Do you think that's God's punishment, Pastor?"

Father is holding the bicycle with both hands on the handlebars, all hurry now blown away. He looks at Mrs. Brogren, who is breathing heavily and mournfully. He looks thoughtfully down the slope toward the river and the fiery sun in the dark water. Then he turns his eyes back to the distressed woman.

"No," says Father firmly. "I'm convinced Strömberg the mission director is wrong. God is not punishing you and Olsson for such a transgression — if it is a transgression at all. God is not small-minded. It's just unfortunate that he allows his parishioners to be so stupid and narrow-minded. But if those thoughts worry you, Mrs. Brogren, you could perhaps talk to Mr. Olsson. I'd be happy to marry you if some decision is made. Just drop me a line. I'm in Dufnäs. Well, you know that."

The fat woman nods several times and swallows, unable to say anything for a moment. She just nods: Yes, I'll speak to Olsson. I'm going to the hospital on Thursday when the relief comes from Leksand.

"Good-bye, then, Mrs. Brogren."

"Good-bye, Pastor."

Pu bows silently and clambers up on the carrier. Father puts his right foot on the little bar sticking out of the hub of the back wheel and swings his left foot toward the pedal. That gives them a good start down the slope toward the river. Pu holds on to Father's hat and extends his legs. He must watch out for his feet.

Far away they can hear the freight train hooting; otherwise the summer day is perfectly still. There's a strong smell of cow and thyme. Straggly stalks of rye lean over the edge of the road and scratch Pu's bare legs.

Pu senses that Father is cheerful, so he is himself cheerful. Father begins to whistle, then to hum, and finally he sings:

> Of wealth of leaves the branch is full,
> the earth covering its dark soil
> with beautiful green clothing.
> The lovely blooms galore
> with greater beauty and glory
> than Solomon delight you.

Father slows down. The road bends sharply to the right and is suddenly sandy and slippery. We'll have to be careful here so we don't go head over heels. You'd better hold on tight if I wobble. Give me the hat. I might as well put it on so I don't get sunstroke. Pu holds the back of the carrier with both hands. Father pedals cautiously. You certainly have to watch out here, says Pu knowingly. If we tip over, that'll be the end of us.

Once Pu and his father have successfully passed the dangerous spot, they cruise at good speed down the gentle slope along the river. The wheels hiss and crackle, the dark water glimmers, the logs float leisurely and pile up at the barrier chains. Beyond the hills, the wall of dark clouds has risen a few finger widths. Father sings to himself and pedals assiduously. Pu doesn't recognize the tune; perhaps there is none. Father is in a good mood for the moment, that is clear, but a journey with Father is always a delicate enterprise. You never know how it will end. Sometimes his mood is good all day, but sometimes, without your knowing why, the demons catch up with the pastor, and he turns taciturn, distant, and irritable.

"You don't regret coming on our excursion now, do you, Pu?" says Father, interrupting his humming and patting Pu on the head.

"No," lies Pu, thinking with loss about his train and rails and the line they were going to lay on the path from the privy to the sawed-off birch. It would have been downhill all the way, and you could couple a set of cars and let them run on their own and they would make their way right down to the switches and pretend they were the electrified Djursholm train.

Several carts are waiting at the ferry, and some churchgoers, who greet Father, and he raises his hat and returns their greetings. A bent old man in a leather cap and a dirty cow with muck on her sides are also waiting. Both are smelly and being courted by big blue flies, but that doesn't seem to worry them. Some boys roam about barefoot on the edge of the water. They are going to Djuptjärn to swim and fish for perch.

Steel cables are suspended across the river. The ferryboat is fastened to the cables by iron hoops and

121

rusty running wheels, the whole ferry maneuvered by hand. The male travelers grasp the cables with gripping devices made of tarred wood, and in that way the flat-bottomed craft is hauled back and forth across the dark, swift-moving current, at this place in a deep notch of the river where floating logs thump dully against the sides of the ferry.

Father at once falls into conversation with two women sitting in a trap, the younger in the traditional parish costume, the older in mourning, and gray and pale beneath her suntan, looking down quietly at her spotted hands. It is the younger one who talks, in a lively dialect that sounds like uphill and downhill. Father nods and listens: Oh, really, did it happen so quickly? That was unexpected, wasn't it? Yes, he was so fit and helped with the hay harvest, and he was off to a shooting match, yes, last Sunday. And when Mother went up with coffee, he was lying there with his head turned to one side and his eyes closed, so Mother thought he'd gone back to sleep. But he was dead.

Pu sits down on the wooden floor right up at the front. He takes off his sandals and lowers his feet into the water, icy cold even now in high summer. The water sucks at his legs and feet.

As the ferry sets off from the swaying pontoon by the bank, Father leaves the two women in the trap and picks up one of the chunks of wood, clamps it onto the cable, and helps the other men haul the ferry through the current and the floating logs.

Pu wriggles even farther out onto the front edge of the ferry and lets the water cool the itching mosquito bites behind his knees. Suddenly someone grabs his shoulder and hurls him backward, then hits him hard, then again. Father is furious: You know I've forbidden you to do that! Don't you realize you can be pulled under the ferry and no one would notice you'd gone? Then another savage blow, three in all. Pu stares at his father. He doesn't cry, not in front of strangers. He doesn't cry, but he is filled with hatred: That goddamn thug who's always hitting, I'll kill him when I get home, I'll think out a painful death, he'll beg for mercy.

The logs thump, the water gurgles, the sun blazes, and his head and eyes are smarting. Pu goes to one side but so that he can be seen. The women in the trap noted the incident, nod and whisper, the young one talking. Pu doesn't hear what she is saying, as he can see them only from behind, where he sits in the stern. Father is helping haul the ferry, struggling with the heavy wooden grapple. He's also angry, Pu can see that. Father has taken off his jacket and rolled up his shirtsleeves, his hat on the back of his head.

Yet another flashback in the future.

"What have I done wrong?"

Father is at his desk. I'm in a shabby leather arm-chair farther back in the room; outside, a sharp gray shadowless winter's day, snow on the roofs and snow in the air. Father turns his face to me, the dark contour outlined against the rectangle of the window. I can distinguish his features only with difficulty, but I hear his voice clearly.

"What have I done wrong?"

The same question over again, and what can I answer? One of Mother's diaries is lying on the desk.

"I've opened Mother's other safe-deposit box and found some more diaries. Can you imagine, Karin kept a diary from March 1913, when we married, until two days before she died. Every day."

"Did you know she kept a diary?"

"I asked now and again, and Karin said she used to make a few notes on things that had happened, but not that — "

Father shakes his head and leafs through the open brown book: *Every day.*

"I try to read them and make them out, I mean literally. Mother uses such tiny handwriting. I have to use a magnifying glass."

Father holds up the magnifying glass as if apologetically: every day, microscopic handwriting, codes.

"Mother's handwriting was otherwise clear and easily readable. But this is different. And she uses

abbreviations of words as well as names. And sometimes there's some kind of code word that is quite
impossible to make out."

Father draws a deep breath and hands me the
book. I get up and take it. Nineteen twenty-seven:
Mother in hospital, a major operation, womb, ovaries
removed. Three months. Worry about home and children. Father visiting every day: "I can't ask him not to
come. I get so tired of his anxieties. As if I ought to
have a guilty conscience because I'm lying here."

I read slowly and with the help of the magnifying
glass, close the book, and push it back across the desk.

"I read and read. Gradually, I am realizing that I
have never known the woman I lived with for over fifty
years."

Father turns his head away and looks at the falling
snow and the white roofs. A bell in Hedvig Eleonora
Church rings distantly. The back of Father's neck is
high and narrow, his hair thin. I know nothing, he
says.

"Karin talks about a fiasco. A life fiasco. Can you
understand that? She writes here: 'Suddenly one day I
read a phrase in a book. It was "life fiasco." It took my
breath away, and then I thought that "life-fiasco" was
exactly the right term.' "

"Mother was dramatic sometimes," I attempt.

"And then I ask myself," says Father slowly and

almost inaudibly, "and then I ask myself what I did wrong."

"But you and Mother must have talked to each other."

"Yes, indeed. We talked, all right. That is, Karin talked. For what was I to say? Karin had so many ideas about how we should change our life. She wanted me to answer her questions, but what could I answer? Karin said I was lazy. Well, not lazy at my work but lazy — well, you know."

Father turns his face to me, though I can't see his expression because the light from the window is so strong, but his voice is pleading: say something that explains this, something that gives me something to hang on to.

"Last night I dreamed Karin and I were walking along the street here. We were holding hands. We did that sometimes. Beyond the edge of the pavement was a precipice and, at the bottom, gleaming opaque water. Suddenly Karin let go of my hand and hurtled down the precipice."

"I occasionally imagine Mother is somewhere near," I say hesitantly. "I realize it's some kind of yearning and nothing else, but all the same."

"Yes," says Father. "That's it. First you find that — no, I don't know. I couldn't sort this out. What have I done wrong?"

"How could *I* know that?"

"I seem to have lived quite a different life from Karin. I've never held God accountable. I've always thought that this is how my life became and there's nothing much to be done about it. Perhaps I've been like a compliant dog. Like Sudd?"

Father smiles mournfully. Sudd's spirit pads across the carpet, puts his nose into Father's hand, and gazes at his master with mournful eyes.

"Mother was probably more intelligent than I was. She read a great deal and traveled abroad. I've mostly lived on my feelings and impulses. Though I'm destitute spiritually now. I don't want to make excuses. Don't think I am excusing myself, but when I sit here trying to interpret Mother's diaries —"

"Do you think Mother intended you to read them?"

"I'm not sure. It was kind of agreed that I would die first. A kind of joke, you understand. It was mostly I who . . . but it was obvious. And when I got cancer of the esophagus, that was that; at least *I* thought that was that."

"The most difficult thing was that we were so frightened."

"Frightened?"

Father looked at me with genuine confusion, as if that were the first time he had ever heard the word.

127

"Frightened?"

"We were frightened you would be angry. It always came so quickly, and sometimes we had no idea why you were shouting at us and hitting us."

"You're definitely exaggerating."

"You asked me, and I'm trying to answer."

"I was fairly good-tempered, wasn't I?"

"No. We were frightened of your fits of rage. Not only us, the children."

"Do you mean that Mother ... that Karin was ... ?"

"I think Mother was frightened, but in another way. We learned to evade, to lie. Though I must say I think it's rather embarrassing talking about this now — two elderly gentlemen. Rather comical too."

"But Mother was certainly not one to say nothing."

"Mother mediated and went between. For instance, Father, you were always angry with Dag. I remember the beatings you gave him. With the carpet beater. On his bare skin. Which bled and peeled off. And with Mother watching."

"You're reproaching me — "

"No, I'm not reproaching you. I'm saying I think our conversation is comical. But you asked me, and I am answering. We were *hideously* frightened, to express it dramatically."

"I remember Karin saying . . ."

"What did she say?"

"When she was angry, she sometimes said I was 'cramped.' That's in several places in her diaries. 'Erik is implacable. Erik can never forgive or overlook, and he's a priest. Erik is unaware of himself.' "

Father, overwhelmed, crumples at the desk. He puts his hand to his cheek.

"I've had my punishment, haven't I?"

"Punishment?"

"Don't you think it punishment enough to sit here at my desk, day after day, reading Mother's diaries? She even complains about my sermons." Father smiles sarcastically. "So you and your brother and sister should be pleased. Some people believe hell is here on earth. Nowadays I'm inclined to agree. No, no, no. Are you leaving already?"

The ferry lands silently, water washing over the planks, the pontoon bridge wobbling, the carts driving ashore. Father says good-bye to the mother and daughter in the trap; the boys going fishing in Djuptjärn take their fishing rods and yell at Pu, who is sniveling: they are sure to have noted that Pu has been beaten and is also on the way to the service in Grånäs. The old man and his dirty cow plod on up the slope.

"Come along, fathead," says Father in his friendly voice.

Pu looks away. It is tempting to cry when Father sounds friendly. He comes over and pokes Pu in the back.

"You must see I was frightened. You could have drowned without anyone noticing anything."

He nudges Pu again. Father stands behind his son, the bicycle propped against his hip.

The ferryman has started letting passengers on board for the return trip. Father holds out his big hand as he leans the bicycle against the safety fence. Then he sits down on an upturned tub and pulls Pu to him.

"I was frightened, you see. If you're frightened, you get angry, you know that? I hit you too hard. It just happened. I didn't have time to think. I'm sorry about that. You got more than you deserved, and that was stupid of me."

Father looks challengingly at Pu. Now it's his turn. Pu doesn't want to look at Father and swallows his tears: dammit to hell, when Father's that friendly, all you want to do is blub, and it's so damned awful. So he just nods: yes, I see.

"Let's go, then," says Father, slapping Pu on the backside. He says good-bye to the ferryman and hauls the bicycle over the slippery boards and the pontoon jetty. A school of small carp are darting around in the shallow water by the shore, then they whisk off, all at the same time, and the surface of the water sparkles. Pu is barefoot. Father fastens his sandals to the back carrier and tightens the leather strap around the suitcase.

The slope up from the ferry is steep. Pu helps push the bicycle. At the top, the heat rises like a wall, and they come out onto open fields and the sandy road stretching straight and narrow to the west. The fine dust spins around in brief whirlpools, without cooling. Father's black trousers, held by the bicycle clips, are gray with dust, his high-laced boots also dusty.

Father and Pu arrive at Grånäs Church just as the bell is ringing. The churchyard is shady; some women in black are watering the flowers on the graves, weeding and raking. A thin cool pervades the porch. The churchwarden, who has been ringing the bell by hand, now takes Father to the sacristy, where there is a washbowl and a can of water, soap and towel in a cupboard. Father strips to the waist and washes, then opens the case and takes out the clean white shirt, his collar, the starched cuffs, and his cassock. The churchwarden rummages about.

"When you get up in the pulpit, Pastor, you mustn't forget to turn the hourglass. It's an old custom in this church, and then we usually say prayers for the deceased *before* the tolling of the knell. I wait for your

131

Amen, Pastor, then I get the big bell going. That takes a few seconds, because she's rather slow. The minister said, by the way, that he would look in to wish you welcome, Pastor, but he said he might be a little late because he had to officiate at communion up at Utby. In that case, he would like to remind you, Pastor, that there's coffee at the parsonage after the service. Perhaps you could tell me the hymns now, Pastor, then your boy can help hang up the numbers. I ring the bell at ten to eleven, and people then usually come into church. Otherwise they're inclined to stand around talking in the drive before it starts."

Father has written down the five hymns and the number of verses on two bits of paper, one for the churchwarden and the other for the organist. The old gentleman beckons to Pu and takes him by the hand. Father has seated himself at the big oak table and is head down over his neatly written sermon. We mustn't disturb the pastor now, whispers the churchwarden, pulling Pu with him out of the sacristy. Do you know your numbers? he asks, opening the black cupboard where the brass numbers are hanging in neat rows.

The churchwarden stands on a small ladder and tells Pu the numbers, and Pu fetches them out of the cupboard and hands them over, to be hung up on the two gold-framed black notice boards to the left and right of the chancel. There is no question of any conversation. The task is important: a wrong number would be a catastrophe.

When the task is complete, Pu goes out of the cool church into the heat, which is slightly subdued by dark, shady elms. The sky is white, not a cloud, breathless, heavy. Some bumblebees, a mosquito on his arm, a cow lowing beyond the stone wall. A few churchgoers in black Sunday clothes are walking along the raked gravel of the paths, talking quietly. Pu moves slowly toward a small square stone building in the north corner of the churchyard. The heavy tarred door is slightly open. No one in sight. Pu knows perfectly well what kind of place this is, but he can't stop himself. He slinks in and stands inside the door: stone floor, rough brick walls, wooden roof held up with thick beams, low windows you can't see through. At the far end, a simple altar with a painted black cross and pewter candlesticks, an open Bible. Shelves along the right wall, on them four coffins of different sizes and execution. A catafalque in the middle of the floor, on it a lidless white coffin tilted steeply toward the door, inside it a young woman. Her face is thin and gray, dark shadows around the eyes, the nose markedly protruding, a psalmbook under her chin, two silver coins on her eyelids. Her hands, long, emaciated hands, holding the psalmbook, a lace handkerchief, and a white carnation. Some flies bounce against the uncovered face, then against the white translucence of the windows. A smell of wilting flowers and something sweetish that penetrates your nose and skin and remains for several hours. Pu stands there a long time. A fly alights on his lips, and he hits out at it in panic.

Footsteps and voices on the path. Two men in dark suits and white scarves plod in, shooing Pu aside but not really taking any notice. The coffin lid is to be screwed down and the flowers collected up. A dirty cloth is drawn across the coffin shelf, the candles on the altar are lit, the doors opened wide, and those attending the funeral assemble for a brief farewell before the service.

"Ah, there you are, Pu dear," cries the minister's wife, beckoning. She has a huge stomach, which she carries before her. She ought to have a little wheel under her stomach. Her flowery dress is tight, and she has liver spots on her face and her sunburned neck. She is holding her son by the hand. "Hello, Pu dear. I've just been in to see your father. He said you were around somewhere. This is my boy, and he's exactly the same age as you. You're just eight, aren't you? Konrad will be eight next week. There you are, Konrad, say hello nicely to Pu."

Konrad is smaller than Pu but broader across the shoulders. His stomach sticks out, but not like his mother's. His hair is as yellow as straw, his eyes are blue, with white lashes. His hands and forehead are wrapped in bandages with pink spots on them. Konrad smells of disinfectant. The two boys greet each other without enthusiasm. The mother says brightly that after the service, Pu and Konrad can play together. They will be given juice and buns, and they really don't have to join the church coffee hour, much too long and boring for two little monkeys.

Before Pu has been able to gather his wits, the church bell starts ringing, and the minister's wife takes him by one hand and Konrad by the other and sways into church, right up to the parsonage pew. I need to pee, whispers Pu in embarrassment. Hurry then, says the minister's wife, letting him past, and it's a squash getting by that vast stomach. Pu rushes around to the north side of the church.

After he has relieved himself, he looks about him. There are only a few gravestones there, overgrown and at all angles. Pu knows why. The Last Judgment will come from the north and knock down the north church wall, so they bury only suicides and malefactors on that side. Their resurrection isn't all that important. They can have the church wall fall on them, as they're going to hell, anyway.

The bell ringing has died away, and the organ is pumping out the entrance hymn. Pu trots diffidently up the aisle. The door to the sacristy is opened by the

churchwarden, and Father comes out in his cassock
and a black silk cloak that flares as he sweeps in. Pu
hopes Father won't see him, but that's a vain hope.
Father sees everything, and he now sees Pu and raises
his eyebrows, though smiling slightly at the same time.
We're friends, Pu thinks. That big black-clad man is
actually *my father.* All these people — not terribly
many — are waiting for Father to speak to them and
perhaps reprimand them. Pu pushes his way in next to
the minister's wife.

Father is at the altar with his back to the congregation, then he turns and sings: Holy, holy, holy is the
Lord of Sabaoth. All the world is full of his glory.

Pu sinks into a semitorpor, squashed between the
wall and the minister's pregnant wife. He couldn't
care less — the service is so boring it's almost incom-
prehensible. Pu looks around, and what he sees
keeps him alive: the altarpiece, the stained-glass window, the murals, Jesus and the robbers in blood and
torment. Mary leaning toward Saint John: "Look
upon your son, look upon your mother." Mary Mag-
dalene, that must be the sinner; have she and Jesus
been screwing? In the west vault of the church sits
the Knight, loose-limbed and bowed. He's playing
chess with Death: I have long been behind you. Close
by, Death is sawing down the Tree of Life, a terrified
jester sitting at the top, wringing his hands: "Are

there no special rules for actors?'' Death leads the
dance to the Dark Countries, holding the scythe like
a flag, the congregation in a long line behind and
the jester slinking along at the end. The demons
keep things lively, the sinners falling headlong into
the cauldrons, Adam and Eve having discovered their
nakedness, God's vast eye squinting behind the Forbidden Tree, and the Serpent wriggling with mali-
cious glee. The flagellants proceed along the south
window, swinging their scourges and wailing with the
mortal dread of sinners.

Pu must have dropped off for a moment, as Father
has suddenly flown up into the pulpit. He is reading
the gospel text for the Feast of the Transfiguration of
Christ: And Jesus taketh Peter, James, and John his
brother up into an high mountain apart, and he was
transfigured before them. And his face did shine as
the sun and his raiment was white as the light. And
behold, there appeared unto them Moses and Elias
talking with him. Then answered Peter, and said unto
Jesus, Lord, it is good for us to be here: if thou wilt, let
us make here three tabernacles — one for thee, and
one for Moses, and one for Elias. While he yet spake,
behold, a bright cloud overshadowed them, and behold, a voice out of the cloud, which said, This is my
beloved Son, in whom I am well pleased; hear ye him.
And when the disciples heard it, they fell on their faces

and were sore afraid. And Jesus came and touched them and said, Arise, and be not afraid.

Pu can't contain his imagination. It explodes into a vivid picture: The scene is Dufnäs hill, right at the top, with a view over the village, the river, the heath, and the hills. Pu is standing on a stone — no, he is hovering a few inches above the stone, his sandals not touching the moss. He is wearing his father's nightshirt, which falls right down to his ankles, and his face is illuminated like a light bulb. Behind him is a cloud, circular and blue-black. In front of him are Dag and the Frykholm brothers. They're staring stupidly and are frightened. The thundercloud splits open, and a light hurtles through the gap, a voice thunders through space, and it is like Father's voice as it cries: This is my beloved Son, in whom I am well pleased; hear ye him. The thunder roars, and the white light goes out. Dag and the Frykholm brothers fall to the ground and hide their faces in their hands. Pu goes over to them and says gently: Arise, and be not afraid.

After the service there's coffee at the parsonage with the churchwarden, his asthmatic wife, and some members of the Grånäs sewing bee. Konrad and Pu are at a special children's table with black-currant juice and buns. The minister, who is nicely rounded, with white false teeth and thick glasses, leans over the boys and gives them permission to leave this ecclesiastical gathering.

"I've got eczema," says Konrad informatively. "I've got it on my hands and scalp. It itches all the time, but it's worst in the summer."

Konrad opens the door to his nursery and looks at Pu with a challenging expression: Well, what do you think of *this?*

The room is equipped as a chapel, the windows with colored tissue paper glued to them. There's an altar at one end, with a seven-branched brass candlestick and an open Bible. Above the altar is a colored illustration from some Christian magazine, framed with gilt beading. A few unmatched wooden chairs are lined up in the middle of the floor, and a small chamber organ with scores and hymnbooks crouches in one corner. Framed prints of biblical scenes hang on the walls. There is a smell of disinfectant and dead flies.

"What do you think?" says Konrad.

"Could we open a window? There's a damned awful smell."

"No, you can't, because then the tissue paper would tear. Shall I give a sermon, or shall we have a funeral? I've got a coffin in the closet."

Konrad opens the door to a cubbyhole full of all kinds of junk, and there indeed is a child's white coffin with a lid.

"No, thank you," says Pu politely. "I don't want to play church service or funeral. Actually, I don't believe in God."

"You don't believe in *God*? Then you must be an idiot."

"God's a piss and a shitty god if you think of the way he's done things. It's you who's the idiot."

"Are you saying I'm an idiot?"

"Anyone believing in God has got a screw loose, you and my dad and all the rest of them."

"Shut up with all that."

"Shut up yourself."

Pu and Konrad start shoving, then they spit at each other. Konrad hits Pu in the chest. Pu retaliates with a blow that displaces the bandage on his head. They take to wrestling. Pu quickly realizes Konrad is the stronger and allows himself to be felled, but that's not enough for Konrad. He sits astride Pu and dribbles saliva, not exactly spitting but drooling.

"I give up," says Pu.

In Dufnäs, that's a signal that the victor is acknowledged, and hostilities cease. In Grånäs, the rule does not apply. Konrad stays where he is and starts twisting Pu's arm. Admit that you believe in God, says Konrad.

"You're hurting me," whimpers Pu. "Let me go. Let go!"

Konrad does not let go. "Admit you believe in God."

"No."

"Admit it."

"No."

"Then I'll have to keep twisting your arm until you do admit it."

"Ow, ow, go to hell —"

"Admit it, then."

"Ow! I admit it."

"Swear by the cross that you believe in God."

"I swear by the cross that I believe in God."

Konrad gets up at once, tugs at the bandage on his head, and scratches violently. Pu sits up. His nose is bleeding, but mildly, only a few drops.

"Anyhow, it's scientifically proved that God exists," Konrad drones. "Some old Russian called Einstein says he has glimpsed God in his mathematical formulae. Huh?"

But Pu fails to reply. He chooses to despise his adversary in dignified silence. The antagonists sit down and sulk, one in each corner. Pu finds a copy of *Allers Family Journal.* Konrad scratches his eczema, picks his nose, puts whatever he finds into his mouth.

Departure is marked by a heartfelt relief that is very much dictated by the unpleasantness of their being together. Freedom is an illusion, and a mild exhilaration oxygenates the blood right down into the smallest ramifications of the arteries. Father takes Pu's hand and is his most amiable self. The minister holds the bicycle and helps fasten on the suitcase. Thank you for a beautiful and rousing sermon. Thank you for your good coffee and good company. Come and see us in Dufnäs. That would be nice for both Karin and me. Won't you stay for dinner after all? It looks as if the weather's turning nasty. No, thank you, we've promised to be home before four and have to catch the train at Djurås. But the storm? The rain may be really terrible after the drought. A shower may well be quite cooling. And we won't melt, will we, Pu? What? says Pu, his mouth open. He hasn't been listening; he is wondering how he can get back at Konrad but can't think of anything. Well, we'll be off, then. Good-bye. Good-bye. Say good-bye to Pu, says the minister's wife to her sourly glaring son. Good-bye, then, says Konrad. If you believe that God exists, then you're dead stupid, whispers Pu, and quickly clambers up onto the front carrier.

So they set off down the parsonage drive. The minister and his wife wave. She grasps Konrad's right hand and makes him wave too. Father raises his hand but does not turn around. He is whistling. Pu holds out his legs, and they make good speed down the gentle slope.

"Now we'll get us a Pommac at the store, and then

we'll go for a swim in the Svartsjön and have our picnic. I suppose you're hungry?"

"I was careful not to eat her awful buns," says Pu. "I kept thinking about the Pommac and our picnic."

"Good for you," says Father, patting his son's linen hat.

The village store is a ramshackle two-story building, the wall covered with advertisements for White Bear (washes while you sleep), Augustsson's Chest Lozenges, Eye Cocoa (two madly staring eyes), the magazine *Pastimes* (a laughing old man with false teeth), and, of course, Gnome Polish and Pommac.

Father knocks on the locked outer door with its windowpanes, a white blind pulled down saying "Closed." After a wait, they hear noises and dragging footsteps, the blind is drawn aside, and the Hunchback of Notre Dame shows his deformed face. When this terrifying creature recognizes Father, his face is transformed by an inviting smile, the key is turned, and the door opens.

Customary greetings are exchanged. The storekeeper disappears, limping and bobbing, behind the counter and opens the icebox in the storeroom at the back. He brings in two misty bottles of Pommac and puts them on the counter. Father asks him how he is. The old man scratches his thin beard and says there's a storm coming, he's felt it for several days. The only advantage of a back like mine is that it predicts the weather, you see, Pastor.

He has put his scarred hands flat on the counter; his nails are curled up under his fingertips and dark yellow. Despite the smell of salt herring, spices, and leather in the store, the stench of the storekeeper's breath hovers like a sharp note of a flute above the aggregate redolence of other smells.

"Perhaps the boy would like a few sweets?" the old man suggests.

"I don't really know," says Father, looking at Pu. "His mother has forbidden sweets because they ruin your teeth. Though, of course, a small twist."

The old man raises his greasy cap and swings it around: Shall be, shall be. He lifts down a glass container full of colorful sweets and neatly makes a cornet out of brown wrapping paper. Then he leans the glass cylinder toward Pu and opens the lid. Fill it yourself, young Mr. Bergman. Stop, and thank you, says Father. That's far too much. What does this feast cost? That'll be fifty öre for the Pommac, Pastor. The sweets are thrown in. Father takes out his big purse and puts two twenty-five-öre coins down on the counter.

"It'll be good to take a dip now," says Father, swinging off down the turn to the lake, a small winding path running through a pasture where some cows are dozing in a cloud of flies and horseflies. The path races downward through a thick deciduous forest and ends in a narrow sandy strip of shore. The Svartsjön is circular and is as black as its name implies. Down there it smells of acrid bracken and rotting reeds.

Father and Pu undress and throw themselves backward into the icy-cold water, Father snorting and waving his arms about, then turning over and swimming off with great splashing strokes. Pu takes things rather more cautiously: you never know with a lake like this. Down there, several thousand feet below the surface, there are sure to be eyeless monsters, slimy horrors, poisonous snakelike creatures with sharp fangs. And then all the skeletons of animals and people who have drowned over the centuries. Pu does a few strokes, the clear, faintly brown water closing around him. He lets himself sink below the surface and can see no bottom, only a darkness far away down there, no water weeds, no small perch or carp, nothing.

They sit on the shore to dry off. The shadows of the birches and alders provide almost no cool, and they are surrounded by clouds of bugs. Father's shoulders are straight, his chest is high; strong long legs and large, almost hairless genitals. His arms are muscular, with brown patches on the white skin. Pu sits between his father's knees like Jesus hanging on his cross between God's knees on the old reredos. Father has found a clump of tall yellow flowers with red spots on them. He carefully pulls apart one of the perianths.

"This flower is called King Karl's scepter — *Pedicularis sceptrum carolinum* — and it's very rare this far south. I think I'll try to take a few of them with me and press them in my herbarium. No, that probably won't do. I can't very well put them in my case; they might stain my clothes."

Father eases a little pea out of the inside of the flower. He puts it into his mouth and chews thoughtfully.

"If you eat the seeds of the scepter, your head starts to spin and you at once start speaking foreign languages, though that's probably just a fairy tale."

Father carefully puts the examined plant to one side.

The day darkens, and a dusty gray cloud appears above the dip of the valley. Some wasps make an assault on the Pommac bottle and the remains of the sandwiches. Suddenly innumerable circles appear on the smooth mirror surface of the water and vanish almost at once. Far away they hear a long-drawn-out rumble. The wind has dropped.

"The storm's coming," says Father with delight. "Perhaps we'd better be on our way."

When Pu and Father have at last emerged from the forest onto the plain with its large open fields, they see perpendicular flashes of lightning inside the bank of clouds above the hills, and the roar, though still far away, is getting nearer. Heavy drops of rain fall into the dust on the road and make streaks and patterns. Father seems unworried. He is whistling some popular old song and pedaling away. They're making good headway.

"This is how we should go around the world, Father and I," says Pu. Father laughs, takes off his hat, and hands it to Pu to look after. Pu and Father are in a good mood. They are fighting the world and not afraid of the storm.

"I'm a Sunday's child too," Father says suddenly.

Up the hill by a deserted village, the hailstorm starts. It has blown up in a minute or so, lightning flashing through the blackness and claps of thunder becoming a deafening roar. The heavy rain is turned into lumps of ice. Father and Pu set off at a run toward the nearest abandoned farm. There's a decayed wagon shed with a few derelict carts in it and a wagon with its shafts up in the air. The roof is all holes, and the rain is pouring in like a waterfall, but under what had once been the fodder loft they find shelter and are also out of the wind.

They sit on a fallen beam and look out through the open doorway. A high birch just down the slope is twice struck by lightning, thick smoke rising from the trunk and the heavy foliage swaying and twisting as if in torment, the claps of thunder shaking the ground and making Pu cover his ears. He is sitting close to Father's knee. Father's trousers smell wet, and Pu's hair and face are wet. He wipes his face on his sleeve.

"Are you frightened?" says Father.

"Suppose it's the Last Judgment?" says Pu suddenly, turning his pale face to his father.

"What do *you* know about the Last Judgment?" says Father, laughing.

"The angels blow their trumpets, and a star called Wormwood falls into the sea, which is turned to blood."

"If that's the Last Judgment, then it's just as well we're together, isn't it, Pu?"

"I think I have to wee," says Pu. He gets up, shivering, and goes behind a wall. He can see Father's back. Father has dug out his pipe and is filling and lighting it.

The gusts of wind, which were at first warm, have suddenly grown cold and hard. When Pu returns from his mission, Father takes off his jacket and wraps it around his son.

One last flashback into the future.

Date: March 22, 1970. Father is dying. He is peri-

odically unconscious with brief moments of con-
sciousness. I am standing at the end of his bed, and
Sister Edit is leaning over him. A night lamp is on,
covered with a thin shawl. The watch on Father's
bedside table is ticking busily. A tray of mineral water
and a glass with a straw. Father's face is greatly emaciated, the face of Death.

"The professor says Father is unconscious, but
that's not true. I hold his hand and talk to him, and
then I can feel him giving my hand little presses. He
hears and understands what I'm saying."

Father opens his eyes and looks at Edit, recognizing her and moving his head slightly. She gives him a
drink of water. Your boy is here, she says quietly and
penetratingly.

I go up to the head of the bed, and Father turns his
head. His face is in shadow, but I can see that his gaze
is strangely clear. He lifts his hand with a great effort
and fumbles for mine. After a few moments of silence,
he starts speaking, at first only moving his lips, but
gradually his voice comes back. I can't make out what
he is saying. He speaks jerkily, his speech slurred, as
the clear gaze regards me steadily.

"What's he saying?" I ask Sister Edit. "I can't make
it out."

"He's blessing you. Can't you hear? Peace be unto
you . . . in the name of the Holy Spirit . . ."

149

It affects me swiftly and unexpectedly, and I have no defenses. Father has closed his eyes, apparently exhausted by the effort, and he sinks back into a torpor. I free my hand and go out into the dining room. It is in darkness and so resembles the dining room of my childhood, with its three windows and heavy green curtains, the dark-stained table, the elderly bulging sideboard with its dully shining utensils, the dark, gold-framed pictures and high-backed, uncomfortable dining-room chairs. I stand at the end of the table, dry-eyed and anguished. Sister Edit opens the door: Am I disturbing you? No, no; don't turn on the light. It's all right like this.

Sister Edit goes over to the window and looks down at the silent, snowy street. She folds her arms across her chest, her face calm. Then she turns to me.

"Why are you so anguished?"

"Anguished? I feel nothing at all. A little compassion, a little tenderness, a slight fear of death, nothing more. After all, he is my father."

"It's probably difficult to feel anything on an occasion like this. That can happen to anyone."

"I don't mean that. I look at him and think I ought to forget, but I don't forget. I ought to forgive, but I forgive nothing. I could have felt a little affection, but I can't bring myself to feel any affection. He's *a stranger*. I'll never miss him. I miss my mother. I miss her every single day. Father is already forgotten. I don't mean the dying person in there — I don't really know him at all — but that man who has played a part in my life: he is forgotten and gone. No, in fact that's not true. I *wish* I could forget him."

"I must go in to him. Are you coming with me?"

"No."

"Good-bye, then, and take care of yourself."

"I wish I didn't feel like this."

"You can't help your feelings."

"You mustn't — "

" — be angry. You must realize that Erik is my dearest friend, has been ever since my childhood. To me, he is quite a different person than he is to you. I don't know the person you talk about."

Edit nods and smiles slightly. I stay by the dark gleaming table. I hear Edit's voice through the closed door.

There is reason to add a note that has scarcely anything to do with this story, as the scene described above was enacted over twenty years ago. My relations to Father changed almost imperceptibly. With a barely endurable movement, I thought about his gaze as he struggled up out of twilight country and called down God's blessing on his son. I started delving into my parents' earlier life, my father's childhood and upbringing. I saw a recurring picture of pathetic effort and humiliating adversity. I also saw consideration, tenderness, and profound confusion. One day, I was able to see his smile and the blue gaze that was so friendly and trusting. I saw Father as aging, severely handicapped, a self-appointed isolated widower: Please don't feel sorry for me, please don't waste any of your time. You must have more important things to do. Please leave me in peace. Things are excellent for me in every way. Thank you, thank you, that was nice of you, but I prefer not to, it looks really awful with my fumbling hands when I'm at the table.

He is amiably dismissive, well cared for, shaven, neat, his head shaking a little, and he looks at me with no pleading or self-pity. I hold out my hand and ask him for forgiveness, *now,* today, at this moment.

Father takes off his jacket and wraps it around Pu. It is warm from Father's body warmth, almost like a hot damp compress. Pu is no longer cold.

"Not cold now, are you?"

"No, it's warm."

The landscape has been obliterated behind a curtain of rain. The hail has stopped, but the hailstones are still on the ground. Outside the shed, a lake has formed and is beginning to pour in under the stone base, so they are soon surrounded by water. The light is gray and flickering, like dusk with no sunset. The thunder is moving away and has a duller note, just as continuous but more frightening. The downpour changes into persistent steady rain.

Father and Pu leave. The road has become racing streams and is heavy going. Suddenly the front wheel skids. Pu draws up his legs and rolls down a grassy slope. Father remains lying on the road. When Pu gets quickly to his feet, Father is lying motionless, with one leg under the bicycle and his head bent forward. Pu realizes Father is dead.

A moment later, Father turns his head and asks Pu if he has hurt himself. Pu says he has got rather wet, as he landed in a puddle, and clownlike, he flaps the long sleeves of the jacket. Father laughs his cheerful friendly laugh, and disentangling himself from the bicycle, he gets up. It turns out the back tire is punctured. He laughs again and shakes his head. We'll have to do the rest of the way on foot now, little Pu.

It's quite a way to the railway station. Father and Pu are wet, dirty, and muddy. Father has a scratch down his cheek. It goes on raining, and the rain is cold. Father pushes the wrecked bicycle, and Pu helps.

Ingmar Bergman's career as a movie director spanned nearly forty years, during which he made such masterpieces as *The Seventh Seal*, *Wild Strawberries*, *Smiles of a Summer Night*, *Persona*, *Cries and Whispers*, and *Fanny and Alexander*. Since his retirement from film-making, he has been more active than ever. He continues to direct in the theater, and his stagings are acclaimed and produced internationally. He has written two volumes of autobiography, *The Magic Lantern* and *Images: My Life in Film*, and two novels, *The Best Intentions* and this one. He also wrote the screenplays for the movies that were made from his novels.